nition

Also available by the same author

Wild Child

Virtual Sexual Reality

Love. in Cyberia

CHLOË RAYBAN

Terminal
Chic

    e-mail

RED FOX DEFInitions

A Red Fox Book
Published by Random House Children's Books
20 Vauxhall Bridge Road, London SW1V 2SA

A division of The Random House Group Limited
London Melbourne Sydney Auckland
Johannesburg and agencies throughout the world

First published in Great Britain by The Bodley Head 2000

This edition published by Red Fox 2001

1 3 5 7 9 10 8 6 4 2

Printed and bound in Great Britain by
Cox & Wyman Ltd, Reading, Berkshire

Papers used by Random House Group Ltd are natural, recyclable products made
from wood grown in sustainable forests. The manufacturing processes conform
to the environmental regulations of the country of origin.

The Random House Group Limited Reg. No. 9540009

www.randomhouse.co.uk

ISBN 0 09 940362 5

I

This isn't how it's meant to be. Love. It should be like that guy in the Armani ad gazing into my eyes longingly, while our lips oh-so-almost meet. Or that bloke in the Highland Spring ad getting ever so hot and passionate with me in the local launderette. It shouldn't be just me, all alone, lurking by Daddy's Apple Mac like some saddo, praying for an e-mail.

An e-mail! A measly little message in a crummy typeface with all that grotty bilge they print before it. It's hardly hearts and roses, is it? It's hardly the kinda stuff you're going to tie up in a ribbon and keep in your bottom drawer for your kids to find and be deeply moved by when you're dead. I must be losing it.

Franz (Francesca), my bestest friend, is philosophical about the whole thing: 'I know you, Justine, I reckon you should've made yourself more available,' was her attempt at a diagnosis. Typical. Franz is Year Twelve's sexual pioneer – she's charitably testing out the ground on the male side of the planet and seeing if it's safe for the rest of us to move in. She's always telling me I'm way too understated.

Max (Maxine) takes a different line: 'Let's face it, Justine, you were being way too obvious. If males sense the merest whiff of female desperation, they make for the hills.' Maybe she's right. Maybe I should've waited for him to make the first move . . . and the second . . . and the third. Oh god, I know she's right.

Henry (Henrietta) is the scientific one among us. Now you can rely on Henry to give a totally objective and balanced view. Henry's got this theory that it's just one big gene pool out there. The ultimate aim of all females is to claim the best male in the pond – the one with the fittest body, the maximum brain cells and the coolest taste in trainers. She delivered the following in a flat monotone that really got to me: 'It's obvious, isn't it? According to your account, he's older, he's smarter, he's got looks to die for and the coolest friends. He even plays in a band. You gotta face facts, he's way out of your league, Justine.'

You know, sometimes I wonder if I even want to be friends with Henry.

The only one who truly understood the situation was Chuck. He said: 'Those surfers think they own the universe. Forget him, Justine.'

I slumped down on his bed.

'Maybe he's just playing hard to get,' I suggested.

'Playing hard to get? Let's face it, Justine, he *is* hard to get. That guy comes from the future. And not just a little way ahead. Another *millennium*. Think about it.'

Had I been thinking of anything else? (No, literally. I know you're not going to believe this, nobody does. But Los, this dream of a guy I met last year, comes from the Fourth Millennium. I never could work out how many years ahead that makes him, but it's yonks. Anyway, despite all that, we really hit it off. Fancied each other like mad. At least I think we did. In fact I know I did.)

'That doesn't stop me being in love with him,' I countered.

'In love. Love! You must really want to make your life a misery. If that guy's in love with anyone, it's himself.'

'But he really liked me. I know he did. He actually made up a song for me. It must have taken him hours. Why else would a guy want to do that?'

Chuck turned back to his monitor, where he'd spent the past day doing an Internet search for my long overdue General Science project. 'It has been known,' he muttered. 'I think it's called "the Justine effect". Makes males act in a totally inexplicable way.'

I felt considerably up-cheered by that.

Chuck really understands me. I've known him since I was born. Before, actually, if you count womb-to-womb contact. You see, Chuck's mother and my mother met each other in antenatal classes at Queen Charlotte's Hospital. They spent a considerable number of our formative hours laid out like beached whales side by side doing breathing exercises. I'd never have known Chuck otherwise. I mean, we're like on totally opposite sides of the social spectrum. He goes to a comprehensive and his friends wear a different set of labels. But being born on the same day and everything, it's like we're kind of un-related twins. And think of all that star stuff. Same day, same place? Short of being born in the same bed we could hardly be closer, could we? Which makes me really doubt horoscopes. I mean, we're *so* different. You can practically guarantee we'll have opposite opinions on simply everything.

'Anyway,' he continued. 'He's just a pathetic loser, if you want my opinion.'

I ignored this comment as predictable male rivalry. 'It must be love. It really hurts. I get a great big lump in my throat whenever I think about him. It's ghastly. I haven't felt this bad since our cat ran away. If only we weren't so far apart.'

'Yeah well, right now you've got to accept the fact that he's

3

currently "out of the scene".' Chuck said this with a most unsympathetic snort of satisfaction. Then he added with a sigh, 'But knowing you, that probably adds to the attraction.'

'What d'you mean?'

'Well, he's unobtainable, isn't he? Means he can't put a big toe wrong. You've made up this great big idealised picture of him, in which he's absolutely smegging perfect. And since he's not around, he's not likely to do anything to disprove it.'

'But Los *is* perfect.'

'Justine. He's even got a crap name.'

'Los Angeles,' I sighed. 'I think it's so-oo cool. Suits him . . .'

'You're not going to blub again, are you?'

'Have you got a hanky?'

Chuck got up and slammed a box of Man-size down in front of me. 'Honestly, Justine.'

'I'm sorry.'

'Have a good blow.'

'Hug, please?'

'Better?'

'Mmm.'

Chuck was right, of course. I gave myself a good talking-to on the bus home. I was totally out of line. He'd put his finger on it. This thing I had about Los was all a big illusion that was feeding on itself. The more I thought about him the more illusive he got. The memories of him were going round and round in my mind like some mad mental spin-dryer until they got worn out. Already they were fraying at the edges. Now all I could remember were little fragments: a look here, the shape of the back of his neck, the cute way he frowned like a pained Alsatian when something puzzled him, the smile lines round his mouth when he came up close. And some of these were

4

fading. He was like some impossibly beautiful jigsaw with pieces missing. And those missing pieces, which I had to make up, made him even more perfect.

I knew I was never going to get the guy out of my system until I could see him again in the flesh. But pursuing a male as far away as Los (a whole millennium away, which is, hang on, erm, yeah, a thousand years) is not a task a girl should take on lightly.

Mummy was pruning in the conservatory when I got home. She's got a new green gardening apron, matching gardening gloves and a green wooden trug to put the bits in. They came from the General Trading Company and they cost a fortune.

'Any messages?'

'Only the usual. Henrietta, Maxine, oh and Francesca twice. I do wish you'd let them know when you're going to be out.'

'I don't know why you can't use the answerphone like any normal person.'

'Some of *my* friends might want to call.'

'Well, you can always override.'

'Don't try and blind me with science, Justine.'

I decided to ring Franz in the vain hope of sympathy. Well, she's still my best friend – although she borrows all my clothes and trashes them, owes me loads and wouldn't think twice about blowing me out if there's a whiff of aftershave within sniffing distance – but no one's perfect.

'Still nothing?' she asked in a callously disinterested tone.

'How did you guess?'

'You've got your "entombed" voice on.'

'I can't understand it.'

'C'mon, Justine. He's not the only male on the planet.'

'He's the only one with yummy blue eyes and kinda weird but gorgeous hair and fit pecs and that way of looking at me like . . .'

Franz broke in: 'You're wallowing again.'

'I rang for sympathy.'

'No deal. You're slipping back. You were starting to get quite positive yesterday.'

'Was I?'

'Yeah, you even agreed to come out clubbing on Friday with the Pack. On the look-out for a replacement.'

'I'm not so sure about it now.'

'How d'you think you're gonna get over him if you don't find a substitute?'

'I don't want a substitute. I want him.'

'I think you're forgetting what we agreed. No retreads, Justine.'

'Yeah well, I hadn't met Los then.'

'Look, face facts, you're on to a loser. He dumped you, didn't he? Made off with his mates and left you stranded? Without a second thought.'

'Not exactly . . .'

'Remind me. What was it he was claiming as an alibi? That he was a time-traveller? Give me a break.'

'But he was. I mean is. You just don't understand. That's why he's so different. You can't judge him by the same standards as ordinary guys.'

'How convenient.' I could tell by her tone Franz's sympathy was wearing pretty thin.

'Anyway, no one can replace him. Other guys bore me rigid.'

'You're a lost cause.'

'I know.' (Sniff.)

'I'm not even talking to you in this mood.'

'Yes you are.'

'No I'm not.'

I heard the click as Franz cut herself off.

I knew what the problem was. Franz was revelling in the idea of having me back, nice and freshly single. Hot for pursuit. All geared up for a man-hunt. That's how the Pack worked. We'd all get dressed up and hyped up Friday night. Perfect down to the last detail – legs waxed, teeth flossed, every eyelash curled and then we'd prowl down to the Admiral Hockerington – cool watering-hole somewhere off the King's Road. As darkness fell and the prey came down to drink, we'd hover, let them get some bevvy down them and establish a false sense of security. Then we'd single out one or two (not the weakest but the fittest) and home in. Few males have been able to resist the combined onslaught of the whole Pack. Basically, I'm not going to be modest about this – when the four of us were in action, males were meat.

I rang Max.

'OK. Let's think positive. You're still playing hard to get. That's good,' she said.

'What's good about it?'

'You're staying cool. You haven't given in.'

I made no comment.

'Justine?'

'What?'

'You haven't, have you?'

'It was only one tiny e-mail.'

'But you promised me.'

'I know. I had a weak moment. We'd run out of Coco Pops.'

'Honestly, I give up on you.'

'He probably hasn't even seen it.'

'What did you say?' Max asked with a sigh.

'Not telling you.'

'It was *that* bad?'

'I only kind of suggested – um – since it was such ages – he might get in touch . . .'

'Amplify.'

'Oh, I just said I'd like to hear from him, something like that. Can't remember the exact words.'

I didn't dare admit the full truth to Max. How I'd pleaded, grovelled, humiliated myself. In verse too! Los must think I'm such a loser.

'Well it's done now. You can't erase an e-mail.'

'I know. I know.'

'Are you coming out on Friday?'

'Yes. No. Don't know.'

'Nice to hear you being so decisive,' said Max and rang off.

I rang Henry.

'I've done something really stupid.'

'So what's new?'

'I e-mailed him.'

'Oh, you're not still going on about your pathetic surfer?'

'Mmmm.'

'You don't mean to say you believed all that stuff about him coming from the future? That guy's a nutter.'

'No he's not.'

'Well you are, then. You make a good pair.'

'If only . . .'

'But you haven't heard from what's-his-name for – what? Must be practically a year by now.'

'Los, and it's forty-nine weeks, ten hours and thirty-three minutes to be precise. I've been logging it up on Daddy's Psion.'

'You are unbelievable. That guy is having you on. A

time-traveller, pur-lease. He's probably having a good old laugh at your expense with his mates right now.'

'Los isn't like that. The last e-mail he sent me – it was so-oo sensitive.'

'Oh, very New Man.'

'Well he is, as a matter of fact. Very new indeed.'

'Look, Justine, let's get one thing straight. You *can* live without men. Girls are brighter, more versatile, better at most things. No – correction – better at *everything*. Look at the statistics. We're coming top of all the exam league tables, we even read at an earlier age. We even *read*! What the hell do we need males for – apart from procreation?'

'Recreation?'

'But why does it have to be this particular one?'

'Henry, listen. This is serious. This time I think it's the real thing. No, not think – I *know* it is. It's *love*.'

This statement was greeted with a sigh of resignation. 'Definition of the "L" word, please?'

'Oh ask me something *really* simple.'

'Come on – supporting evidence, then.'

'It must be love. I can't get him out of my mind. I keep having all these flashbacks . . .'

'You make him sound like a car crash.'

'How can you be so unfeeling?'

'Accept it for what it is. Obsessive behaviour, Justine. Let's face it – what you need is therapy.'

'Ugggh!'

I hung up this time.

Oh why had I sent that message? It was so-ooo naff. The little hairs on the back of my neck stood on end with horror every time I thought about it. And I'm not going to admit what I put – even to you.

How was I ever going to overcome the humiliation?

I sat in front of Daddy's Mac, searching for inspiration. It had its big dumb screen-saver face on. I put my tongue out at it and caught my reflection as it was flung back at me.

But maybe there was a solution. I could always send another message – something which would cancel out the first one. I considered tactics. I needed to up my status, make myself somehow more desirable. *Competition* – the oldest ruse in the book. Nothing like it to bring out the red blood in a guy. Henry was right, he wasn't the only male in the world. Maybe if this was pointed out to him . . .

I logged on and tapped in the password. With a fresh e-mail page before me I hesitated, searching for those magic words that would transform Los from 'Unavailable' to 'Inseparable'.

Darling Los?

Dear Los?

Los?

Nope. From now on 'cool' was my middle name. I typed in simply:

> Hiya!
> How's it all going?
> Ignore everything in my last e-mail. Some ghastly mix-up with my English homework. Aren't those romantic poets pa-the-tic? Talking of romance, I'm taking Franz up on that bet of hers. To see who can get off with the most guys by Christmas. Currently having the coolest time hanging out with bloke number seventeen.
> If you wanna get in contact I'll be staying over at his place mainly at: http://ourworld.compuserve.com/ webwonderstud/cnd

OK, so it was Chuck's e-mail address. Wonderstud – pur-lease!

Still, Los didn't have to know that, did he?

I checked through the message. That should do the trick. And then I sent it. Off it went, winging its way through space and time. So that was done. I hoped it made him nice and jealous. I hit Quit.

Hang on. What was that nasty little message on the screen?

Some messages in the Out Basket have not been sent.

Pur-lease!

Do so before disconnecting?

I selected **Yes**.

Another crap message came up:

Messages successfully sent: 1 of 2.

I double-checked Los's web address and sent the message again. But Dad's dumb, dated technocrap wasn't up for it. It just wouldn't co-operate. It kept bleeping back at me and coming up with pert little tight-lipped messages about an 'illicit web address', whatever that might be. I spent another ten fruitless minutes fuming over alternative ways of typing Los's address but the Apple Mac wasn't having any of it.

I resorted to stabbing angrily at those mysterious and seldom-visited keys that lurk round the edges of the keypad. I'd seen Chuck do crafty little things with the Apple and esc keys. I was sure I could fix it. Then out of the blue, the Mac had the cheek to ask in a nasty ironic manner:

Do you want to Quit?

Did I want to Quit? No, actually. I wanted to send that e-mail. I saw red at that point.

You've heard of road rage, haven't you? Well, this was the information superhighway version. Techno rage – mindless fury directed towards a persistently and, I reckoned, *intentionally* malfunctioning piece of technology. Computers have been flung from great heights for less.

'Call yourself a PowerMac?' I said, gritting my teeth. 'I'll show you who's boss around here.'

Six 'oh-no' seconds later I realised I'd wiped everything. I checked back, with my palms going damp and my heart pounding. Oh no, oh no, oh no! All Daddy's website files had gone.

I was in deep ★★★t, man.

I rang Chuck.

I tried to explain in plain English what I'd done.

Chuck made some amused and dismissive noises and then suddenly switched into 'Help-Line' mode and made some totally unfathomable enquiries.

After five minutes of this I was reduced to a kind of mental jelly. Technically brain-dead.

'Why don't you just reboot?'

'Re-what?'

'I don't believe this! Try turning the mains switch off and then on again.'

'Sure it won't blow up?'

'Justine!'

I did as he said. Magically the files reappeared.

'You're a genius.'

'I know.'

'Why do you understand all this and I don't?'

'I guess I'm just more evolved, that's all.'

I did go out with the Pack that Friday night. It seemed it was National Cheer Up Justine Day and there was no backing out. We'd raided the cashpoint, planning to make an extra special night of it. And we'd managed to slip out early from school so that the four of us could engage in a little retail therapy on the way home.

As I slid my body into a new pair of Calvin black jeans, I was starting to wonder if Henry hadn't been right about the therapy – it did seem to help. A little further down the King's Road I added on a pair of the newest chunkiest Adidas Airflo trainers and at Baby Gap I notched up the teeniest-weeniest T-shirt I could squeeze my Wonderbra into. Y-esss!

Eight p.m. found us in the 'Ad Hoc', leaning up against the bar.

'So,' said Franz. 'What do you fancy?'

I cast an eye over the choice of male on offer. There were a load of boys freshly released from boarding school who smelled as if they'd been sheep-dipped in their older brothers' aftershave. A group of rough that might have had potential in one corner – had they not been busy bawling at a football match on the telly. And the usual embryo city types still in their suits.

I sighed. 'Not a lot.'

Franz raised an eyebrow at Max. 'What do we do? Force-feed her vodka till she lets her standards drop?'

'No way, she'll only get maudlin. We'll select for her. We know her tastes.'

'Umm, s'like arranged marriages, you know – they can work brilliantly,' Henry agreed.

'Look, guys, I'm perfectly happy on my own, OK? Stop hassling.'

'How about him?' demanded Max, homing in with laser accuracy on a quite cute guy who'd just pushed through the doors.

'Too short.'

'He's OK.' Franz pointed out a boy in a tight Calvin T-shirt who was manhandling a one-armed bandit with the ferocity of a kick-boxer.

'Overworked, look at those pecs. Can barely get his arms down by his sides. Looks like Popeye,' I pointed out.

'Or him?' Henry zoomed in on an intellectual dweeb in steel-rims.

'Oh pur-lease.'

In the end, the entire Pack gave me up as a lost cause and concentrated their efforts on three guys who, judging by their readiness to pay for drinks, were so well-heeled their feet hardly touched the ground. Max let drop in an undertone that the three of them were more than happy to take us along to Mycene later.

I was not impressed, so they left me propped up against the bar talking to a guy whose complexion suggested he lived on pizza.

'So what do you do, then?' he asked.

I was obviously looking well beyond my calendar age. Well, I had made an effort. I didn't want to admit I was still at school, so I said, 'Nothing much.'

'Oh? What d'you live off?'

'Daddy, mainly.'

This had a very positive effect. He offered to buy me a drink. I decided to make him suffer for his mercenary instincts and ordered a Bellini, which is *the* most extortionate concoction made of champagne and peach juice. After that he obviously thought he'd purchased me for the evening and clung like mud.

'You two seem to be getting along,' whispered Franz, who by now had prised the kick-boxer from the one-armed bandit and was starting to make forays outside with him for a breath of fresh snog.

I made desperate signals from behind pizza-face's back, but Franz was too preoccupied with her conquest to take any notice.

Max wasn't any more help. She'd homed in on the cute guy whom I'd dismissed earlier on as too short, but then Max isn't that tall herself.

Pizza-face was just getting round to asking where I'd been

on holiday this year and my eyes were positively glazing with boredom, or it could have been the Bellini – anyway, everything was starting to feel kind of distant – when my mind swung back to Los again.

Oh if only he wasn't so-oo far away. I was never bored with him. Even though he was so deeply into technology that I didn't understand half of what he said. But there were such aeons between us, what did I expect? The difference just made him that much more fascinating . . .

'Justine? That is your name, isn't it?' Pizza-face had noticed my slip in concentration.

'Oh yeah, sorry.' I'd finished my drink. He was leaning ever closer towards me. I'd had enough of this. 'Look, there's a friend of mine over there. Why don't I introduce you?' I suggested.

I'd singled out the most stunning girl in the room. Ash-blonde hair, legs to die for, and a cleavage that was currently acting as the local male magnet. Yep, sure enough, P.F. had seen it.

I grabbed him by the arm and led him over.

'HI!!!!' I said, giving her a couple of miu-mius on the cheeks. 'I haven't seen you in *ages*! You are looking *stunning*!'

'Hello,' she answered doubtfully.

'Look, I've got to introduce you to . . . Umm, Gareth, oh, Gary. He's been dying to meet you. Back in a mo – simply bursting for a pee.'

I caught up with Max in the Ladies.

'Look, I gotta get outta here. If that loser gets any closer his total lack of cool might rub off on me.'

'It's fixed. Those three guys we started out with are bringing their Merc. round to pick us up. We've just got to pick up Henry and extricate Franz and we're off.'

'Actually, I think I've had enough. I'll make for home.'

'No deal,' said Max. 'Tonight was meant to bring you back to the land of the living, remember?'

'But, I really don't feel like . . .'

'No backing out now. You're coming with us.' Max practically frogmarched me out of the Ladies.

It was getting near closing time and the place was filling up with guys who thought they could capitalise on other fellas' spending power and secure girls without having to splash out on drinks.

Eye contact was enough to bring Henry squeezing her way out through the massed bodies to where we were poised by the door.

Franz was more difficult to shift. She was splayed out on the Ad Hoc's wall with her kick-boxer clamped to her. In the end we settled for taking them as a pair. Well, there were only three other guys anyway.

I sat trapped in the back of the Merc., squeezed between a guy who reeked of Armani with Max on his lap and Franz and her kick-boxer who'd moved on to pawing and giggling. London nightlife slid by. I gazed out of the windows, catching sight of bits of boys who looked a bit like Los. God I felt miserable.

'Cheer up, Justine,' whispered Max. 'There's bound to be talent at Mycene.'

The boys who'd brought us forked out wads of cash on the door and we were in. Talent? Predictably, the best-looking guys in Mycene were the perma-tanned boys who manned the place.

We went downstairs to where hip-hop was playing. A selection of girls in teeny skirts and high, strappy sandals were dancing to it. There weren't, in actual fact, any guys around. At the bar, more girls with perfect Jennifer Aniston hair and minimal cocktail dresses were eyeing us condescendingly –

blatantly trying to demoralise us so they could move in on our escorts.

The others settled at a table in a corner and Henry squeezed over and patted a seat beside her. I took it and sat gazing at the decor, desperately trying to summon up some Friday night-ishness. All the festive red plush and gilt was having a demoralising effect on me. Why was I the only one not having a good time? A really doleful-looking stuffed zebra head on a plaque kept catching my eye.

'Drink?' asked one of the boys, shoving a glass in my hand and filling it with bubbly. I exchanged glances with the zebra. His glass eye twinkled at me encouragingly.

'Why not?' As a matter of fact I was feeling somewhat dehydrated and could have killed for a Perrier but I sipped it dutifully.

'Dance?' asked another. Neither the zebra nor I could think of anything against this either.

'Yeah, why not?'

Frankly, if someone had said 'Strip?' or 'Slit wrists?' I probably would have said the same. I don't want to sound melodramatic about this, but my nightlife simply had no meaning any more without Los.

Eventually, I got back home. So much for a great night out, I sighed at my reflection as I passed the hall mirror. God I looked wrecked.

I took off my shoes and placed them dutifully side by side on the stairs and started the silent creep past my parents' room up to my bedroom. Hang on, the light was blinking on the answerphone.

I paused. I didn't want to wake the olds by playing the message back. But on the other hand, would I be able to sleep if I didn't?

I turned the volume down and pressed New Messages.

'Justine!' It was Chuck's voice, and he sounded really odd. Totally freaked out. 'There's an e-mail for you. You're never going believe this. You've gotta get over here, right now!'

2

Chuck was waiting in the doorway as I paid off the cab.

'What's so urgent? Why couldn't it wait till morning?'

I hadn't seen him this excited since he'd got that e-mail telling him he'd broken the all-time world record Gameboy score. (And I swear it wasn't me who set that up.)

'Come on, upstairs!' he hissed.

I paused at his bedroom door. 'If this is some devious plot to get me under your Thomas the Tank Engine duvet . . .'

'Would I?'

'Well you are male. Kind of.'

'Thanks.'

'So amaze me – what is it?'

'Look!'

Chuck pointed to where his battered PC sat on his desk looking like some veteran craft from *Star Wars*. It was positively caked with accumulated dust, the keys were clogged with keyboard lint and the caps lock was secured with a piece of grubby Elastoplast. It blinked at me geriatrically.

'Don't tell me. You've had another hit on your Verruca Concern homepage?'

'Very funny. No. It's an e-mail for you.'

I was across the room in three strides.

It read:

> Venus. You are a star.

(It was Los's pet name for me.)

> I got your e-mail.
> Made me think.
> We ought to spend more time together. How's about my place this time? Next weekend?
> I've booked your trip. Just check in Friday p.m. at:
> Butrav
> Fourth Floor
> 115 Colesworth Rd
> Lewisham
> London.
> They're expecting you.
> So am I.
> When you arrive. I'll be there waiting.
> Los

'Ohhhh!'

'Is that all you're going to say?' Chuck was leaning across the desk staring at me.

'That's just so-oo sweet.'

'Justine. He's invited you to *his* place. D'you know what that means?'

'That he really cares about me after all?' My eyes were filling with tears, I couldn't stop them. Brimming over with joy this time. I felt light and bright and slim and beautiful. I felt ready to conquer the world. Right back to my old self, in fact.

'Justine. Think about it. *His* place.'

'I know. I'll probably meet his family and everything.'

'But *his* place.'

'Oh-my-god what shall I *wear*? No, I know, thank goodness I bought those Calvin jeans. Next Friday! I gotta check through my wardrobe!'

I was already on my feet. Chuck got between me and the door. He held out his arms to stop me leaving.

'Justine, think about it. You'll be travelling into the *future*. To a place and time that hasn't *happened yet*.'

'What – you mean black Calvins could look totally dated?'

'I don't think you've thought this through.'

'You're right, I haven't. I'll have to make up something to tell Mummy and Daddy.'

'Is that all you can think about?'

'It's OK. Brilliant! Franz has asked me to go on this dweeby sailing trip in Norfolk with her dad. It's meant to be a real father-daughter bonding session. But she's begged me to go too, in case he gets on to heavy issues – like her overdraft and . . .'

Chuck slumped down at his desk and put his hands over his head. 'I just don't believe you sometimes.'

'No. It's a really good excuse. We'd be totally out of touch. He's banned her mobile, so there'll be no telephone contact or anything . . .'

'Justine.' Chuck was talking to me very slowly now. 'He's asking you . . . to travel to . . . the year . . . 3001.'

'Mmmm. I know.'

'Just think of the implications.'

'Like what?'

'Like . . . you're travelling to a place where everything is going to be light years ahead. I mean, three thousand and one! It's so-oo far ahead.'

I came back down to earth. 'Umm. Well, when you put it like that. Yes. I guess it is a bit scary.'

'Scary! It's mind-blowing. Think of what you could find out, technologically, mathematically . . . I mean, in theoretical physics, for a start . . .' Chuck had suddenly switched into science-speak, his voice was positively shaking with emotion. 'They'll have cracked the complete unifying theory of the universe by then . . . They're bound to've done. They're not so far off it now. I mean, you could find out stuff that would upstage Stephen Hawking . . .'

'Bor-ing! I'll have better things to do than search out reams of nerdy physics and stuff for you . . .' (What should I wear on my feet?)

'It's not reams. It's no more than a string of symbols – one little equation. You could simply look it up and e-mail it to me.'

'You know what I'm like with numbers and stuff. I can't even type in an e-mail address without messing up.'

Chuck had moved on into dream-mode. 'I could get an A – no, a double A in Physics A-level. I could get into Oxford . . . or Cambridge. I could become the youngest Physics prof ever. Justine. Think about it.'

Chuck was practically hyperventilating from excitement. He'd gone down on his knees, and looked as if he was about to propose or something.

'I'll do anything, *anything* for you in return,' he pleaded.

I smiled indulgently. 'Would you invite me to one of their cool balls? You know, the ones where you all end up totally out of it, in a punt at dawn?'

'I'll book the punt right now! Look, you don't have to worry about a thing. I'll be your back-up. You need never be out of touch.'

'Promise!'

'You'll do it, won't you? You'll go! You'll get it.'

'I might.'

'You will?'

'I'll think about it.'

So that was why I was in South London, of all places, on a bleak Friday afternoon. I'd gone there straight from school. Lewisham – I didn't know such places still existed.

I'd had a bit of trouble sorting it with Franz. I knew I'd never in a million years convince her of where I was really going. So I tried something marginally less unlikely. I pretended I was staying the weekend with Chuck.

'*Chuck?*'

I ignored the contempt in her voice. 'Is my memory playing tricks? Or did I imagine that time when you took him "in hand", as you put it?' I countered.

'I really can't remember.'

'Well, with all the boyfriends you've had, baby, it's hardly surprising.'

She didn't register the barb in my voice, she took this as a compliment. 'So you'd really prefer a weekend with "mouse-potato" rather than cool cruising with me and my dad?'

'Boats are so damp. It'd just be one long bad hair day.'

'Well, if you think it'll help get that cyber-freak out of your mind.'

'I think it might help sort all that out – yes.'

'Glad to hear you being so positive. Take care.'

'Franz, not everyone's like you.'

'Whatever . . . And, Justine. Remember you owe me one. For providing cover for your "olds".'

'Don't I always do it for you?'

'You are my best friend. Isn't it part of the job description?'

I searched down the High Street and took the turning into Colesworth Road. I don't think power-jetting could have penetrated as far as Lewisham, the streets were really murky with a kind of matt-black London grime you simply don't see north of the Thames.

I checked the A–Z again. I wondered if Los had made some mistake. This couldn't be the right place, could it? You'd think on a trip like this there'd be a special VIP terminal or something – like for Concorde – all squishy carpets and glossy rosewood – but quite possibly more hi-tech.

I found number 115, a narrow doorway lurking in a dodgy way between shops numbered 113 and 117. Sure enough, above the bell of flat three was a small engraved white plastic plaque which read *Butrav Clinic – Fourth Floor.*

I hesitated for a moment and swallowed. My mouth felt dry. Is this what Sir Francis Drake felt like when he set off in search of potatoes in the New World? (Or was that Sir Walter Raleigh?) Is this what the Apollo astronauts felt like before they were blasted into space like puffed wheat? Did I really want to do this?

I needed to call Chuck for courage but there wasn't a callbox in sight. Oh why had Daddy confiscated my mobile? It was so-oo unfair. Everyone else's parents paid their bills without a murmur. It would serve him right if I never came back. I could picture him with Mummy now, being desperately contrite: 'If only she'd had her mobile with her, this might never have happened.' Huh!

This thought gave me courage.

I pressed a finger on the bell and a reassuringly normal voice answered: 'Butrav Clinic.'

'Justine Duval. Apparently, I'm expected.'

'Oh, Duval J? Yes, right. Push the door and come up to the fourth floor.'

It was a narrow winding staircase fitted with a central strip of worn haircord. The paint was peeling and the air smelled faintly of cats. This wasn't the kind of environment sci-fi films led one to expect. Where was all the matt steel and hi-gloss chrome? The acres of seamless glass? As for 'beaming up', the place didn't even have a lift. I toiled up the stairs to the top floor.

Sure enough, the door up there had a similar white plastic plaque which read: Butrav. There was a buzzer beside it.

I buzzed.

A slot in the door slid open like you see in prison movies.

'Can I help you?'

'I'm Justine Duval. I'm meant to check in.'

'Do you have ID?'

Honestly, this was worse than picking up my cashcard at NatWest. I groped through my backpack and after a lengthy sort through the usual wreckage of hairbrush, blusher, tissues, crushed Marlboro pack, fraying fags, chewing-gum, leaking pen with spare cartridges, Franz's missing leisure club pass – oops! – I located my bus pass. It wasn't a very good likeness. I'd been yawning at the time. I looked like a whale.

'Could you hold it up closer, please?'

I forced a yawn.

'Oh yes. I see now. That'll be fine.'

There was a click of electronic bolts and the door swung open.

Inside was a kind of doctor's reception area. A stretch of squeaky, non-slip, marble-effect lino led up to a semicircular reception desk.

More disillusionment! Where were all the dolly birds in nylon jumpsuits with necklines that fastened in that cool utility clothing way like dental nurses wore? Where were all the lacquered hairstyles and lip-glossed smiles? The woman who'd opened the door had the kind of starched breasts and see-through white nylon lab coat that made me think, ominously, of hospitals.

She introduced herself as Janice and went and sat behind the desk. She gestured to me to sit down on the chair opposite her.

All this hospital stuff was giving me the willies. I hadn't felt this nervous since Franz and I nearly had our wisdom teeth out. She'd read somewhere that this would give you that hollow-cheeked Gwyneth Paltrow look and had dragged me along to a cosmetic dentist for moral support. I was just about to be forced into a totally unnecessary, and most probably horribly painful operation, when they discovered on my X-ray (to my intense relief) that I didn't actually have any.

'Just a few formalities. I'd like you to answer some questions and then there's a consent form to fill in . . .'

I swallowed. 'Consent?' (I'd time-travelled before, but into the past last time, and there'd never been any of this kind of palaver. But I suppose as things move on people get paranoid over safety standards. Butrav obviously didn't want to get sued if something went wrong.) Went wrong! A shiver of apprehension ran down my spine.

'Is this really necessary?' I asked.

'Standard procedure,' she said with a tight little smile, passing me a form. 'Don't worry about it. We're the longest-standing operators in Britain.'

('Operators!')

'Shouldn't I have heard of you, then?' I ventured.

'Only if you're incredibly up-to-date,' she said briskly. 'We've only been going . . .' she glanced at her watch. 'Thirty-three minutes.'

'Pardon?'

She smiled her tight smile again. 'You're our very first customer. Aren't you lucky?'

'Am I?'

'Well yes. Everything's brand new, you see. We've only just imported the software. Couldn't be better.'

A glance down the form made my heart sink further. It asked for things like 'next of kin', hardly a reassuring question at the best of times.

'What would happen if something, er, went wrong?' I asked. 'Would you have to tell my parents?'

'It won't. It can't,' she said briskly. 'Everything's been rigorously pre-tested by an independent panel. The equipment is quality-controlled, service-checked, Kite-marked, and meets the 2998 universal-interglobal standards for digital-temporal realignment.'

'I know, but . . .'

'Now, just a few details. Just for the weekend, is it?'

'I've got to be back at school on Monday. If I bunk off sick again I know I'll get suspended.'

'Fine, we'll book you back on Sunday night. Six p.m. OK? I've just a few further things to check. Any history of . . .?' and she reeled out a complete medical dictionary of diseases. I replied automatically 'no' to each. But I wasn't really listening. Now that I was actually on the verge of it, the awful realisation of how risky this whole trip sounded had truly sunk in.

There was still time to back out. And then I thought of Los. Two whole days and *two whole nights* of him all to myself. That was twenty-four plus twenty-four which, makes – errm – *forty-eight* hours of intensive one-to-one exposure. Would that be long enough? Come on – people are said to fall in love at first sight, aren't they? Forty-eight hours was plenty. In fact, it was long enough for it to wear off . . .

'Contact lenses?'

'Pardon?'

'Are you wearing contact lenses?'

'No.'

'Do you have implants?'

'No!'

'False teeth?'

'Certainly not.'

'Right, if you'd just like to fill in your details and sign between those two crosses, I think we can proceed.'

After a moment's indecision I filled in Chuck's name and address as next of kin. Let's face it – our relationship was much closer than mine with Mummy and Daddy. Then I took a deep breath and signed the form with a flourish.

'Good. Right.' She pressed a buzzer on her desk.

Another woman, this time in a blue-checked version of the receptionist's lab coat came through the door.

'This is Charmaine. She'll be looking after you this afternoon.' Janice passed over her clipboard with another tight little smile and Charmaine took charge of me.

'Hello, Justine. Will you come this way, please?'

My knees felt weak as I followed Charmaine through a further door. This one was like a safe door, incredibly thick and solid. As we went through, it slid closed automatically with a horribly final-sounding 'thunk'. I turned and hesitated for a moment, staring at it.

'Come along, then.'

Charmaine was already moving purposefully down the corridor, her shoes went squidge, squidge, squidge, on the lino. I followed and caught up with her as she stood, holding back a green canvas curtain.

'In here. Everything off, please,' she said, passing me a gross nylon gown, checked like hers.

'But I can't go in this!' The gown didn't even do up

properly. It had tacky kind of tie-things at the back. Didn't she realise how crucial this was? Meeting Los again was going to be the turning-point in my life, like pivotal. I'd spent hours and hours deciding what to wear. I'd taken every single thing out of my wardrobe and rejected it. At the last minute I'd even handwashed my favourite knickers and had to wrap them in a towel and jump up and down on them to get them dry in time.

'I'm sorry but you simply can't travel in your own clothes.'

'But these jeans are Calvins and these are brand new retro Adidas. They're the latest . . . hottest . . .'

'I hardly think so, not where you're going, dear.' She checked her clipboard. '3001 wasn't it?'

'I'm not so sure about it now.'

'Your watch too, please.'

'This is a Tag.' (I'd leaned on Daddy hard and got a genuine one for my seventeenth.) 'Now if you lose this . . .'

'Don't worry, we keep all personal possessions under lock and key,' she said briskly.

'Oh I really don't know about this . . .'

'I'm afraid it's too late to change your mind. You've signed the consent form and we've already established protocol.'

'I know, but . . .'

'Someone will be there to meet you at the other end, won't they?' She flipped over a page on her clipboard. 'Oh yes, that's right.'

There was a picture of Los on her sheet, staring out at me. My heart did a lurch and changed up a gear. For a moment I'd forgotten how simply, unutterably gorgeous he was. With difficulty I stopped myself from drooling.

'It won't *hurt*, will it?' I asked feebly.

'Goodness me, no. How could it? It's digital.'

I took another lingering look at Los's photo. He was grinning at me encouragingly.

'I won't be a minute,' I said. I slid the curtain across and stepped out of my jeans.

When I re-emerged, feeling horribly exposed at the back, Charmaine was waiting for me. She pushed another, even heavier door and held it open for me.

'In here, dear. If you'd just like to lie down on the bench.'

There was a narrow metal bed thing with a thin strip of disposable paper sheet on it.

I must be mad. Totally, completely, utterly mad. No one in their right mind would be doing this. Which only goes to prove – it must be love. It must be the real thing.

'There you go,' said Charmaine, pushing me down gently by the shoulder and lifting up my feet so that I was forced to lie back. 'Just you relax and enjoy it. It won't take a minute. Now I'll be watching you all the time through that window. As I said, you won't feel a thing . . .' she added with a reassuring smile.

Forget reassurance – she wasn't even going to stay in the room with me. This was definitely unsafe. Forget all the 'boldly going' stuff. I'd never felt less bold in my life. I reckon even being born was a doddle compared to this.

But hang on, music was playing. It was the kind of dreamy soprano voice stuff like they play on British Airways to lull you into a false sense of security.

How I wished I were simply going to Tenerife or somewhere. Even Benidorm would do. If only this was one of those gloriously ordinary holiday take-offs with that nice grainy voice saying, 'This is your captain speaking . . .' It's always the same voice, isn't it? As if the same guy is always out there in the cockpit going endlessly round and round the world like the Flying Dutchman. I reckon they select pilots for their voices – 'Never mind if you can steer, old chap, just talk into the mike for us . . .'

But hang on, something was happening. Panic attack! The music was being interrupted – not by a nice, square-jawed captain's voice, but by an adenoidal electronic one, saying, '*The uploading procedure is about to begin. Please try to stay absolutely still. Do not be alarmed. As the scanner passes over you, it will be taking a digit by digit personal read-out. This will simultaneously be transmitted to your destination. Do not move from your position until the scanner has come to a complete standstill and has been switched off.*'

Move? I was so petrified I'd gone into a kind of living rigor mortis.

Then the music faded in again. And what could I smell? It was Los's favourite aftershave. Los. Sigh! You have no idea how gorgeous he is. I only have to think about him and I totally lose any sense of where I am or what I'm doing. I spent the first half-hour of my latest GCSE Maths retake reliving the last time we met. I was so lost in thought I was under the impression the multiple choice was one of those magazine quizzes – where you tick all those little boxes, like: *Score ten As and it really means he loves you.* So you see, I did have a really good excuse for failing again. Daddy needn't have been so beastly about it.

The music changed. It switched to the intro of one of the numbers Los played with his band. And what were these pictures coming into my mind? Me and him, all sort of dreamy, slow-dancing very close indeed, with a kind of greasy halo round the image. Naff visuals maybe, but in the present circumstances very very acceptable.

With difficulty, I tried to retain a sense of detachment. There was no point in going all weak and helpless over him. I had forty-eight hours to bring the boy to heel. Forty-eight hours. I'd never had a challenge like this before. I gritted my teeth and tried to summon the required degree of positive attitude.

And then his voice kicked in, with that slightly husky tone of his. He was singing the lyrics of the song he'd originally dedicated to me:

'Venus, brightest star on my horizon,
Shine for me . . .'

And I completely lost it.

I was so blown away that I hardly noticed that I was being fed, head first, like the filling in canelloni, into this big metal tube thing.

Whizzy noises started up and these little green and red lights zoomed back and forth around my body. The scanner was taking cross-sections, like cuts made across a tree-trunk so that you can count the rings. But it wasn't just recording rings, it was reading essential parts of me, like liver and kidneys and all those wibbly bits that don't bear thinking about. And it was taking ages over it. I wondered what would happen if I got up now and tried to make a run for it? Would I be able to run? Or since I was only halfway through, would only half of me arrive? I kept pretty still at that thought. Why be modest? My legs are the best bit of me. I wasn't going to risk leaving those behind.

At last the scanner got down to my toes, came to a standstill and fell silent.

So I was scanned. What was going to happen next?

The door of the room opened. But it wasn't Charmaine who came back in. The girl was wearing the same uniform. But this girl was incredible. About six foot tall with a faultless fall of glossy blonde hair, ski-slope cheekbones and blue eyes you could drown in. She shouldn't be slumming it in hospital lace-ups. She should be in five-inch heels, swanning down a catwalk! What on earth was a girl like her doing working in a dump like this? In Lewisham of all places.

'Sprotid olis?' she asked.

'What?'

'Sprotid olis?' she repeated.

I couldn't understand a word she was saying. 'Look. What's going on? Don't you speak English?'

She didn't. She just gabbled on at me: 'Niet. Nat vos Babel Internat Globalspik?'

Gingerly I sat up and looked around me. It was the same room – absolutely the same. But Charmaine had gone from her window. And this girl looked as if she were from a different race.

That's when it dawned on me.

I'd arrived!

3

Another gorgeous girl, dark this time, had come into the room. Forget Naomi Campbell, she could go back to her day job. They both stood staring at me and the first one said to the other, 'Dus bin liner?'

'Ejet sprotid olis, met niet interlucommen.'

'Sprot! Est intellingum erat?'

'Dat. Ist protocol intereglem.'

They were speaking a language that didn't bear any resemblance to anything I'd ever heard before. No, correction, it resembled practically any language I'd ever heard. It was like a ghastly verbal cocktail that included every language from Alaska to Zanzibar. And I'd been so-oo sure the whole world would be speaking English by now.

'Dat.' She checked her file. 'Numen Duval Justine.'

Now perhaps we were getting somewhere. I decided to resort to what Mummy does when she's abroad. Speaking English very loudly and enunciating every syllable, extremely clearly.

'Yes, that's me,' I said.

'Intellingum ma niet Babel sprocken.'

'Look. Listen. A boy. Los. Said he'd be waiting for me.'

They looked at me blankly. 'Los?'

'Los Angeles.'

'Los Angeles, USA metrolopolis niet?'

'Dat. Positive.'

'No, he's a person. That's his name.'

The blonde shook her head, obviously not comprehending.

I resorted to sign language, gesturing wildly to indicate someone tall and hunky.

They both shook their heads.

(That was so typical of him. To promise to be there and then be late. Don't you just hate it when boys do that?)

But then suddenly the dark girl caught on. She started rubbing a place on the wall. I watched as under her hand the wall became transparent. I could see through into some kind of waiting-room beyond.

There was Los, waiting for me, stretched out nonchalantly on a sort of futuristic couch with his arms behind his head, asleep maybe. He was even more gorgeous than I remembered.

'Ident positive?' she asked.

'Oh – ye-es! Positive!'

She let her hand drop and the wall sealed over again.

I swung my feet down towards the ground and stood up slowly.

I felt oddly light-headed. No, I felt oddly light-footed. Come to think of it, I felt oddly light all over.

I swayed and sat down again. Oh-my-god. What had happened? I felt as if I'd lost around twenty kilos. Had I discovered history's most effective crash diet on the way here? Either that or something very very strange was going on, like someone had turned down the dial on gravity. I was positively floating. Where on earth was I? If I was on Earth?

'OK?'

'OK.'

The girls gestured to me to follow them. I walked, or rather half-floated across the room to where they held the door open for me.

On the far side there was another changing cubicle with a similar green canvas curtain. It was a mirror image of the one I'd left. But my nice new Calvin jeans, my pristine tight white T-shirt and my cost-a-bomb trainers were nowhere to be seen.

The first girl was running a kind of gauge up and down my body like they do at Airport security checks. I realised she was measuring me. Good sign. Fit is everything when it comes to clothes.

You fantasise, don't you, about the kind of clothes that'd feature in a future millennium? My version was kind of Issey Miyake with Princess Leia overtones. All flimsy and see-through and minimally body-covering in some kind of futuristic fabric that only clings to you in tactful places and cleverly side-tracks anything like flab or a visible panty-line.

She looked at the gauge and frowned and tutted. 'Negvibe. Sub-optimal,' she remarked to the other girl.

'Sprot?' she asked, checking the gauge. And then she nodded and tutted too. 'Opt droid declamen.'

'Sub-optimal? What do you mean, sub-optimal?' I demanded. I was quite proud of my body actually.

The blonde disappeared and returned after a minute or so holding a kind of dun grey plastic body-bag.

'Oh. You can't seriously expect me to wear that?' I said.

But it seemed they could. The girls came out with what I could only interpret as standard salesgirl patter. They both positively purred at me: 'Bezok grunt lymprocta cojabat optima dat . . .'

The dark girl was holding it up against me. 'Dat. Prim instal guzundit.'

This was ghastly chain store one-size-fits-all clothing taken to its nth degree. No one could be expected to wear stuff like this. And to meet Los, too . . .

'Look, this is really important. Haven't you got anything else? Couldn't I have my own stuff beamed up or something?'

But they both insisted it was this suit or nothing. I sighed at my reflection as the thing was drawn up to my neck.

'Sprot prim,' said the blonde. She leaned back over her measuring gauge and started punching in numbers.

There was a hissing sound like compressed air coming out of a car tyre and all of a sudden I was shrink-wrapped!

I stared back at my reflection. The suit had metamorphosed into one of those all-in-one jobs guys wear for the Cresta Run – makes them look like sperms – all sleek and shiny, clinging to every contour.

I winced. It was really tight in all those tightest places. For someone who'd rejected G-strings on the grounds that they felt like being sliced vertically, this was not a pleasant experience.

'Niet grut?' asked the blonde.

'Very niet indeed,' I growled.

There was a fizz of air and breathing became an option once more.

'Opt dat plus. Opt dat minus.'

'Plus or minus what?'

'Plus . . .' said the blonde, punching in some numbers to let the suit out a bit, 'dom minus.'

Before my eyes my waist took on the kind of circumference I'd fantasised about.

'You mean I could have, like, bigger boobs, smaller bum?'

'Opt plus. Opt minus.' She demonstrated the options again.

37

'Oh boy! Go for it! Er dat?'

It took ten minutes or so for she and I to agree on my ideal proportions. I was all for going the whole Elle MacPherson but she seemed reluctant, so I settled in the end for a kind of Kate Mossy bottom half with a bit more Herzigova on the top.

It appeared that I could also colour the suit however I liked, and the girls and I had a bit of a sign language set-to over the options. They kept switching the suit into really naff shades like swimming pool turquoise or granny's cardie peach. But I insisted on playing safe and going through all the options till we eventually settled on black. Come to think of it, on closer inspection in the mirror, I had actually managed to make the suit look somewhat like the jeans and polo neck that were my standard faves to wear back home. Especially since I'd got my own way about turning the leg-ends into flares. Just goes to show, doesn't it – how deeply formative those fashion influences can be?

The dark girl went off, muttering disapprovingly. She returned with a pair of mules. Quite chilled ones, actually. They had the kind of really thick-ridged soles that were all the rage back home. They weighed a ton. But once I'd slipped them on I felt nicely earthed to the globe once more.

I admired my reflection in the mirror and decided that my new look deserved some make-up. I turned to the blonde and made some making-up gestures in the air.

'You haven't got an eyeliner or a blusher I could borrow, have you?'

'Niet mutilatum visage mit coloratura,' she said in a very prim and proper manner.

'Oh sor-ry,' I said.

And with that she went over to the wall. There was a sound a bit like gin and tonic fizzing and a gap opened just wide enough to let me pass through.

4

He wasn't asleep. He had his eyes closed listening to something – Walkman or whatever, although I couldn't see any headphones.

He jumped to his feet as soon as I appeared and to my intense relief came out with a sentence in perfectly ordinary English.

'Justine! Long time, no see!'

I searched his face for significant signs of deeply felt emotion. Wasn't he meant to look drawn, thinner, a bit paler perhaps? Where were all those care lines? He'd been suffering like me, hadn't he?

Not a bit of it. He looked exactly the same. Perfectly, utterly sickeningly perfect.

I waited, eyes closed, lips poised. This was going to be one of life's most historic clinches . . .

Nothing happened.

I opened my eyes again. He was standing back and looking at me with his head on one side and . . . hang on. He was *laughing*.

'Hi!' I said, suddenly feeling as if I'd grown too many limbs. I tried to put my hands in my non-existent pockets.

In the absence of any action from him, I didn't know whether to kiss him or what. I offered a cheek and felt a delicious brush of his slightly stubbled cheek against mine.

'Hey . . . well! You look, er, *different*!' he said, holding me at arm's length, looking me up and down.

'Do I?'

'Mmmm!' He glanced briefly downwards, taking in my chest. Well, actually, he couldn't avoid it.

I started fervently to wish that I'd allowed the girls to settle on 36B rather than 38D. I tried hunching my shoulders but my chest fought back. Basically those boobs were out to get noticed.

'What have they done to you?' he asked.

'Isn't this what everybody's wearing?'

'Erm, well not everybody,' said Los. He was still cracking up.

'I didn't think this suit was really me,' I said miserably.

'You can say that again.'

This was so unfair – I'd become a fashion victim before I'd even set a foot outside the Terminal.

'Well, how was I to know what people wore here?'

'Oh, some people wear that stuff, all right,' said Los, trying to repress a final smirk.

'If you think it's so funny I'm going to go back and demand they change it. But they're speaking the most peculiar language in there. I'll never make them understand.'

'That's Babel. Globe-Spik. We're all meant to learn it at school. Nobody does.'

I turned back to where I'd come through. Where *had* I come through? The wall had sealed over just as the window had earlier. There was a total blank, featureless surface as if nothing had ever been there.

'It's a time-lock,' said Los. 'You'll need an SDN window

to establish protocol.'

'Translation, please?'

'Won't open till you're due back. Which is, erm . . .' he paused and gazed into space. 'Eighteen hundred hours, Sunday.'

'Can't you do a big persuasion job? This is important.'

He laughed. 'No way. You get a ten-minute time slot and that's it. Miss that and you're stranded here. Time lanes are chock-a-block these days.'

'So you mean I'm stuck dressed like this?'

He put an arm round my shoulders. 'Don't worry about it. We'll go shopping. We'll find you something nice and retro.'

'Shopping?'

Things were looking up.

He led me from the 'lounge' onto the terminal concourse. I'd never been in such a vast space before; made our Millennium Dome look pea-sized.

I followed, trying to take everything in. The air was filled with incomprehensible announcements in Babel. The concourse was teaming with people either making their way in or trying to find their way out, or just standing around in the lost-looking way of people meeting people.

We got caught up in a group of tall Eastern people posing in front of a vast LED which kept flashing up the time, the date, and the year. They waited patiently for me to move on. It took me a second to realise they were videoing the occasion and I was in the way, although I couldn't see any sign of a camera.

'Time-tourists,' said Los dismissively. 'The whole place has been overrun with them since the millennium. All rubber-necking over the most trivial detail. I mean, look at them.'

He pointed to a group which was being herded along

through the concourse by a guide pointing out features with a scarf round her lightpole.

I'd stopped in my tracks. I wasn't staring at the decor. It was the people I was staring at. BOY! Had things moved on!

I'd expected the future to feature the universe's less fortunate individuals, like in the movies. Random aliens with the type of skin you're warned about in cosmetic ads – half elephant hide, half tortoiseshell.

But no. These people were more like supermodels.

Where were all the pointy ears and curiously symmetrical hairlines? What had they done with the normal-looking people? No! What had they done with all the *less* than normal-looking people? The ones with low knees and one-piece eyebrows? Exterminated them?

This couldn't simply be nature at work, could it? Take dogs, for instance. If you started out with a load of pedigrees, and left them to their own devices, 'at it' for a thousand years or so, you'd end up with mongrels, wouldn't you? I mean, like really mixed mongrels. Those ghastly kind of matted black and white jobs with one leg shorter than the other three? But all these people were pure pedigree through and through. The human equivalent of Borzois and Red Setters heading for a great big rosette with Best of Breed splashed right across it. The girls were all of a Miss World finalist standard and there seemed to be an infinite supply of them. They were swanning around in that loose-limbed, aren't-I-a-babe? fashion that showed off the best bits of them – which was most bits. But I didn't have time to linger. Los was forging his way through these babes as if they didn't exist, and I was forced to follow.

Suddenly we broke through the crowd and were out of the terminal. And bonus! I had this really vivid *déjà-vu*. Here it was – *heaven*, as I'd imagined it. The most enormous shopping mall in the universe. I call myself an optimist, but I'd never dreamed the future could be as good as this!

Recently, I've evolved this theory that heaven is one vast celestial superstore. Those of us who've led good and just lives will have infinite supplies of money to spend forever on whatever we like. Hell, of course, is the opposite – the mean and wicked are going to spend eternity in a torment – toiling through a netherworld of car boot sales and charity jumble sales, burned up by excruciating fires of embarrassment about being uncoolly dressed.

But this shopping mall was actually beyond heaven, beyond anything I ever could have imagined. When I say enormous, I mean like kilometres high, endlessly long and filled with infinite buying potential. I paused on the threshold. From every angle colour, sound, logos, numbers clashed in on my consciousness. I looked down – and there was even more of it!

Below me was a mind-blowing drop, more malls going vertically downwards endlessly – it was like that trick picture on my grandmother's biscuit tin that had hypnotised me as a kid. It had a picture of the tin on the top of the tin, which had the same picture on that, so that it went on endlessly getting smaller and smaller forever. Yet this was the real thing and as deep as the Grand Canyon. Or maybe deeper. But instead of layers of fossils, there were layers and layers of shops. Shops, shops and more shops. I wondered if the merchandise got more and more dated and unfashionable as you went down, like all those old dinosaur bones.

Los was getting impatient. 'Come on . . .' he said.

'No, I can't.'

'What's up?'

'You're walking . . . on air!'

He was. Everyone was. Everyone was being whisked along at a ridiculous pace with no visible means of transportation.

Los was the only exception. He was walking back towards me as fast as he could, yet staying where he was.

'No I'm not, stupid. It's transporflor.'

I suddenly realised that he was on a totally transparent conveyor.

He held out a hand. I put one hesitant toe forward. There did seem to be something under my foot – unnervingly see-through and slightly bouncy. I edged outwards and took off.

'I think I'm going to be sick.'

'Don't look down. You'll soon get used to it.'

To my relief I found that, despite appearances, the conveyor was reassuringly solid. I risked another furtive glance downwards. Everywhere, people were gliding up and down, backwards and forwards between the vortex of buildings on what must have been similarly transparent walkways. Basically, you could see why miniskirts had gone out of fashion.

Trying to ignore the quite extraordinary impression that I was walking on air – I mean *literally*, not just because I was hand-in-hand with Los – I strode along beside him.

Everything was highest-of-high gloss, as if the whole place had been put through superwash in a giant dishwasher with a double dose of rinse aid. Everywhere there was a gentle hiss of air-conditioned air that smelled faintly eggy – like it had been recycled so many times you were basically breathing pre-owned breath.

As we zoomed along the mall, I couldn't help feeling a little thrill of possessiveness. Here I was, stepping out with the universe's coolest and most drop-dead gorgeous guy. I noted with satisfaction that the two of us were attracting plenty of attention. Girls kept waving at him or sidling up and saying 'Hi'. And guys kept giving me the once-over and sending Los those little male signals – raised eyebrow, thumbs up,

44

half-wink. A bit obvious, perhaps, but they clearly thought he was on to a good thing. But hang on, why were they noticing me? Compared with the other talent around, at best I'd only rate as a 'maybe'.

We took a side-turning and as we continued we passed even more sickeningly gorgeous girls. All top-notch designer catwalk quality. Regular features, perfect skin, and there wasn't an inside leg measurement under 34 inches. Oh this just wasn't fair. Compared to them I felt like a Cabbage Patch doll that had accidentally been shunted on to a production line of Barbies.

I scanned the concourse for some sort of variety. There weren't any of those funny little robotic dwarves and not a sign of a mutant. In the movies there's always one, isn't there? A great bulbous, globby type with a single glaucous eye in the middle of its forehead, that kind of leers at you.

It would've been a relief to see someone with at least an outsized nose or sticking-out ears – I might have felt less out of place. Even a few of those tubby little yellow-eyed people in sackcloth robes would've been a bonus. But everyone I set eyes on was one hundred and fifty per cent perfect.

God look at those two over there! Correction, two hundred per cent perfect. And the two goddesses in question were directing blatant *come-hither* looks at Los.

He swept past them as if he were immune. Back home, if I was with a guy and we passed any single one of these girls in the street you could be absolutely certain that he'd turn round and check their back view. I mean, he'd be falling over his shoes, bumping into lampposts. But Los didn't even seem to register their presence.

But wait a minute! It wasn't just the girls. It was the guys too. A group passed, laughing and joking together, and I actually felt my jaw drop. Tennis players' legs, athletes' bodies, all-season tans. I mean the kind of talent you can't take your eyes off!

Oh boy – a couple of them were giving me the once-over. Exposure to so many sexual thrills was having a heady effect on me. I smiled back.

Los might think my suit was a joke, but I felt quite proud of my new remodelled body actually. I thought pensively of how much respect I'd get at school with a body like this. My Wonderbra had never been that convincing. At that point, the cutest of the guys – the one with the Matt Damon eyes – took a step in my direction and I half-said, 'Hi.'

'Don't take any notice,' said Los.

(He was jealous – sweet!) I preened myself mentally.

'They think you're a Simchick.'

'A what?'

'A Simchick. A droid – not real.'

'Not real?'

'Not human. Simchicks are like, umm . . . street entertainers. It's the way you're clothed.'

I couldn't exactly picture myself producing a banjo and strumming right here and now, but still . . .

I caught sight of a group of girls dressed the same way as me. Some guys were approaching them and they were pairing off.

'Street entertainers?' I felt myself flushing scarlet. 'You mean I look kind of *cheap*?'

Los gave me a half glance. 'Not cheap necessarily but certainly *available*.'

How could they have done this to me? It was like those nightmares when you walk down the street in your underwear. No, worse. When you walk down the street *without* your underwear.

'Oh my god. This is *so* embarrassing.'

'Don't worry about it. Nobody knows you here.'

'Yet.'

We continued in silence for a while. A girl about my age with long, shiny black hair was dodging along another walkway, staring across at Los. She kept getting caught up in crowds and falling behind. She started leaping up and down and waving as if she knew him. Smiling in a far too friendly manner.

Hold it right there, girl. Los was with me, wasn't he? I quickened my pace and moved in a possessive centimetre or two closer to his body, hoping to establish prior claim.

The girl was a positive siren, the kind of quality that could get a guy to sit through weepy movies with her. She was now rushing down a walkway at breakneck speed on a collision course with us. I flung her a hostile glance.

Too late, she'd already caught Los's eye.

'Oh look, I'd better stop and talk to her I suppose,' he said in a bored kind of way.

'Sure, go ahead. Feel free,' I said, hopefully sounding dead casual.

'Don't move. I'll only be a mo.'

I stepped off the conveyor and stood to one side, trying to appear oblivious to their encounter.

I concentrated my gaze on this massive hoarding. It was like a poster but weirdly 3-D. There was an incredibly lifelike photo of a really cute guy on it. I half-turned to face him, putting on a big act of totally ignoring what was going on on the opposite side of the mall. (That girl was practically rubbing her body up against Los.)

Making a superhuman effort to shift my attention from the two of them, I tried to work out whether the guy on the poster was as cute as Los or not. Which was really, really difficult. Because this guy had a yummy jaw line, the kind you just want to creep up to, and snuggle under and . . . When he *winked* at me.

47

I blinked and rubbed my eyes. This was a poster, wasn't it? Was jet-lag catching up with me, or should I say time-lag? But I was right. He had moved. He was grinning at me in the most irresistible manner.

'Hi,' he said. 'Have you got a mo?'

I cleared my throat. 'Errm . . .'

Well, Los was over there with that girl, wasn't he? And she was sticking to him like fluff to a toffee.

'I can see you're interested,' he continued.

'Well, er . . .'

'Come a little closer.'

I cast a lightning glance over at Los. This was outrageous behaviour! And in the street too. I moved a lot closer.

'Nice footwear – Lo-G,' he said, casting an assessing glance at my mules.

'Yep well, not my choice really. But they're not bad, I suppose.'

'I can see you're a footwear person.'

This wasn't exactly the kind of chat-up line I was used to. But maybe things had changed in a millennium or so. I decided to humour him.

'You've got pretty cool footwear yourself,' I said.

Actually, he was wearing the most hideous moon boots; same kind as Los was wearing. Great big baggy things like people my time wear for *après-ski*. They seemed to be all the rage in 3001.

No sooner had I mentioned this than he started to take me on a minutely detailed tour of his boots. He had one of them off in a flash and was demonstrating how to adjust the soles.

'Hi-G, thru-Lo-G to No-G, just by a flick of these tabs,' he said. 'Cool-conditioned for whenever you go Upside.' And then he leaned towards me and added in a conspiratorial undertone. '. . . and ideal for those trips Downside.'

'Downside?' I asked.

He put a finger to his lips and winked again.

'What do you mean, Downside? I've only just arrived, you see . . .'

But he didn't seem to want to answer. Instead he interrupted with: 'Have you got a mo? I can see you're interested.'

'What are you doing?'

I'd been so absorbed with my fit footwear man that I hadn't noticed Los was back. He was watching me with that grin of his as if I'd done something really stupid.

'Nothing.'

'You were talking to that guy, weren't you?' Los raised an eyebrow.

'Well, what if I was?'

'Don't let me stop you. Ask him something else. Ask him about his T-tank,' he said indicating his T-shirt. 'No, better, ask him about his undergarb.'

The boy on the poster was looking back and forth from one to the other of us, as if uncertain which one to talk to.

'No!'

'Go on. Don't be shy.'

'OK, I will.' I turned to the boy. 'That's a nice T-tank you're wearing.'

'Oh do you like it? It's 100% pure cotton fibre guaranteed for wash and wear over twenty years. Would you like to see the care label?'

I glanced at Los. He gave me a nod.

'Yes please.'

With that the boy started to strip off. No, honestly! He had such fit pecs and such a yummy tanned torso too. If only Franz had been here to see this.

Los grinned. 'Ask him about his undergarb.'

'No!'

'Chicken.'

'And is your undergarb pure cotton fibre as well?' I asked.

And Los added, 'And does *that* have a care label?'

The boy started to undo his belt then paused mid-action and slurred to a halt. 'End of demo, smeg off,' he replied. And with that his clothes magically reappeared. 'Hi, have you got a mo? I can see you're interested,' he started up again.

'He's not real, is he?'

'What do you think?'

I realised I'd made a complete idiot of myself, talking to a poster, so I changed the subject. 'Who was that girl?'

'Oh her. Just a friend.'

'Looked like a pretty close friend.'

'Not particularly.'

'Oh yeah! She was all over you.'

'She was just being friendly.'

'That was more than friendly where I come from.'

'Well, things are a bit different here.'

'So I've noticed.'

'People don't want to own people.'

'Own people?' I swung round and stared at him. 'That is about the most arrogant thing I've ever heard any guy say.'

He shrugged. 'I was just stating a fact,' he said and continued on his way. I swept after him.

'Well thanks for letting me know.'

I was livid. I was fuming. I practically had steam coming out of my ears.

Los glanced over his shoulder and noticed my expression. He stopped in his tracks and waited for me. 'You're not going to be all "Third Millennium" about this, are you?'

'What do you mean – Third Millennium?'

'You're a bit out of date, that's all.'

'Me! Out of date!'

'Only by our standards. It's understandable.'

'Don't you talk down to me.'

'There you go again. Overreacting.'

Perhaps I should explain. Los and I had been down this track before, when we had first met up in my time or what most people would call 'the present'. Los had tried to explain then that attitudes had changed a wee bit over a millennium or so. Like in his time people didn't go in for one-to-one 'relationships'. The whole thing was more kind of easy-going. If you read the signals, you could see things were already going that way back in my time. And I'd tried to be cool about it. And I still was – trying, I mean – not cool.

Los looked at me assessingly, then said with immense male insight, 'You look a bit down. Maybe you're hungry?'

'I am *not* hungry.'

Actually food couldn't have been further from my mind. Since I'd been with Los I hadn't had a single craving. Not even for Coco Pops.

He'd paused beside a glossy booth which had things that looked like cash dispensers in the walls.

'Well *I* am. Come on, you gotta eat something,' he said.

'Eat? Where?' I asked, casting around for something vaguely resembling a restaurant.

'Here.'

'In a bank?'

'It's not a bank. It's a Simulator.'

'Oh right.'

'So what do you want?'

'I don't want anything. What's the choice?'

'Thai, Chinese, Indian, Anglo-Indian, Caribbean, Afro-Caribbean, Spanish, Italian, Indonesian, French, Dutch, Swedish, Irish, Scottish. In a choice of spicy, sweet, savoury, sweet 'n' sour,' he paused for breath. 'Or, if you prefer, you can have a mix of the whole lot.'

'I s'pose I could just about choke down a salad.'

'Salad's dodgy, they haven't quite cracked the technology yet. Comes out kinda limp.'

'I'll just have a taste of what you're having.'

'You sure? You haven't heard all the options yet.'

'I'm positive.'

He leaned towards the Simulator and stared hard at it. A voice droned. '*DNA2FTB. Reading your print. Print accepted. Please select from the menu.*'

'What's that mean? Reading your print?'

'Auto-debit. Eye-print. 'Slike a fingerprint. We're all different. Zap your print and charges are auto-debited.'

'You mean no card, nothing to sign? You don't even have to remember a PIN number?'

'What's a PIN number?'

'Never mind.'

Los started to dictate choices to the Simulator so fast I couldn't keep up: 'Large-hot-vegetarian-organic-white-long-cut-medium-Lo-cal-deep-fry-Lo-sodium-salinated-with-double-sucrose-free . . .'

(A take-away in the street. This wasn't exactly the romantic dinner I'd planned for our first meal together.)

'Do you think we could sit down somewhere?' I asked as he paused for breath after delivering his order. 'My feet are killing me.'

'You want to *sit down* to eat?'

'Well yes. I wouldn't mind.'

'Fine. Anything you say. We'll take a cell.'

(A cell! Sounded *really* romantic.)

He led me down some stairs into a kind of underground booth about the dimensions of an aeroplane lavatory. There was just enough room for the two of us to squeeze in. The table was the diameter of a side plate.

'OK?'

'Fine.'

Los looked at me thoughtfully. 'Maybe you'd like a bit of atmosphere?'

'Don't worry about it.'

'No, it doesn't cost extra or anything. It's just a bit naff, that's all.'

'I'm fine.'

'You would, wouldn't you?' He leaned over and said to no one in particular. 'Flower for the lady, please.'

With that, a rose in a single stem vase appeared on our table.

'Cool!'

I reached out to touch it and my hand went straight through the vase. 'It's a hologram!'

'How about a view?'

'A view?'

'Five star de luxe,' said Los and he winked at me. 'Nothing but the best.'

Instantly soft muzak started playing and the walls of the booth fizzed with static then transformed themselves into what looked like the dining-room of a ridiculously OTT luxury hotel. The place was dripping with chandeliers, and all the diners were in full evening-dress.

'*Would madame care to taste?*' asked a voice.

'Say yes or you won't get served,' said Los.

A 'waiter' appeared to be standing beside our table, holding a silver salver. He placed it between us and lifted the lid with a flourish.

A thousand years had passed and, predictably enough, boys' taste in food hadn't changed one iota. Beneath the lid was a bag of chips and a sachet of ketchup.

The chips were hot, crisp and weirdly bubbly inside, pretty good actually. We were soon fighting over them. You have to hand it to the foodies. There's nothing like a bag of hot chips to bring people together.

As we finished the last chip, the dining-room dematerialised into pixels and the electronic voice droned, *'We hope you've enjoyed your meal and appreciated your luxury ambience. Please tell your friends and call again soon.'*

5

The mall was even more crowded when we emerged.

'Oh, man, look at the crush. Everyone's out of school,' said Los.

'Aren't these people a bit old for school?'

'Not since they raised the leaving age to thirty.'

'Thirty! How simply ghastly!' (Just think of all those extra school years eating into your quality life time. Years and years more of essay deadlines to miss, revision to skimp and exams to fail.)

'I s'pose there must be more history to learn for a start,' I said sympathetically.

'Oh we don't do much history. These times it's more things like A.I. or Eugenics. Then there's Bio-tech, Nano-tech and Neuro-tech . . .'

I listened with a sinking heart as the list grew longer. All that stuff about taking an intelligent interest in your guy's favourite topics had just flown straight out of the window.

'And there's all the languages: Babel, Polyglot, Cybagram. Then there's Old English . . .'

'Olde Englishe? You mean you still study stuff that's like before Chaucer?'

He shook his head. 'No, Old English, the stuff you speak.'

'But I speak normal English.'

He shook his head. 'Uh uh, not here, it's not.'

Our progress kept being held up by friends who greeted Los like a long-lost brother. I tagged along, feeling really out of it. You know what it's like when someone you really have the hots for meets up with old friends? Pre-you friends? The kind that look at you as if you're something they've accidentally trodden on and they're not quite sure if they ought to scrape you off on the kerb?

Well, Los was surrounded. They were all coming up and greeting him with the highest of hi-fives and things like: 'Hey, how goes?' and 'Where were you all day?' 'What's that you're with?' 'Cool droid!'

I stood there, heartily wishing that my dress code wasn't so blatant.

But why should I worry? Los's friends were wearing the weirdest assortment of clothing. Like they'd taken this 'Making a statement' stuff really to heart. Even 'punk' had made a comeback and they'd found places to pierce that no one my time had even thought of. But, since they all had bodies that would make you reassess a bin-liner, of course everything looked sickeningly brilliant on them.

Los, at last, remembered I was standing there.

'Ignore the suit. She's not a droid. Meet Justine. She's here on a trip from the past,' he said by way of introduction.

'Nice to meet you, I'm Rio,' said the guy who'd stopped us. He had on what looked like an orange plastic potato sack with arm-holes cut out. He hi-fived with me. 'Welcome to the Fourth Millennium. When do you come from?'

'1998.'

'You blag?' he said, his eyes narrowing. 'Cryonic! Never met anyone from that farback. Didn't even suss they had

56

access that millennium. That's incredulous!' He turned to the girl beside him. 'Hey, Florence, suss! Is Justine, she comes from the Second Millennium!'

'You kid! That's non-possible!' said Florence. 'Listen to this, Iona.'

'Only just,' I replied with dignity. 'The very end of the final century.'

'The Twentieth? Oh Crion,' said Iona, who was the first person I have ever seen able to make me want a shaven head. 'I've seen vidz of it. Not you all drive round in horses and big pull-pods?'

We were drawing a crowd by now.

'Positive,' joined in a stunning Asian girl with hair twisted into silvery spikes. 'The males wear big headcover and ride horses and have blasters and zap people. The females have these big puffy clothings, they ride round in pull-pods.'

'Negative, that was the Nineteenth,' said Rio.

The fuss was attracting yet more attention. Another guy, Tyrone, a positive Adonis with long blond dreadlocks, had overheard. 'Crion! Farback. Second Millennium,' he said. 'The one with horse-and-pod races, round and round with gladiators and lion-fights too.'

'Negative. That was First Millennium.'

They broke into a heated argument.

I suddenly realised that all their information must be gleaned from their equivalent of archaeology – vintage movies. I decided to try to regain a little credibility.

'My time, actually, everything's terribly hi-tech. We have cars and planes and rockets . . . and . . . basically everything's done by computers,' I said.

They looked at me blankly. 'Non suss, what is a computer?'

I was into a no-win conversation here. I cast a helpless glance at Los.

'Justine's just arrived, needs space.'

'Positive. What doing post curfew? You playing tonight?' asked one of the guys.

'Might be an idea to let Justine settle in first,' said Los.

'You could meet up with us tonight, positive,' said Florence.

'Yeah, why play games when you can connect with us?' complained the girl with the shaven head.

The two of them started a big persuasion job. They'd taken possession of Los. They walked on ahead, one on either side, as if they owned him. The Asian girl with the silver spikes dropped back with me.

'Name's Yoko-hama,' she said. 'Welcome to our time. How long you stay?'

'Just the weekend.'

She was being quite friendly for a mate of Los's. I took the opportunity to do a little research. 'How well do you know Los?' I asked as the others swept him out of earshot.

'He's in our year at school. We meet up in virtual.'

'Has he got a girlfriend?'

She frowned as if she didn't understand what I was on about: 'He has friends. They are girls. Positive.'

'No, that's not what I mean.'

She looked confused. 'What is it you ask?'

'Isn't there one special girl? One he likes best?'

She shook her head so that the spikes tinkled against each other and she laughed. 'All girls here are special. He likes us all.'

She was right there. We'd caught up with the others. Iona and Florence were saying goodbye to Los in a way that suggested I had an awful lot of groundwork to catch up on. Yoko-hama joined in. Iona was the first to tear herself away.

'Prime. Have good time, you two! You two currently connecting?'

'Not yet,' answered Los. 'Justine's not even wired yet.'

'Get her wired. then.'

The three of them made off, waving and blowing kisses.

Los caught my expression. 'Anything wrong?'

'What's all this wired business? And what precisely does she mean by "connecting"?'

'Wired's like "on-line". And connecting, erm, I think, your time, you used to call it "shagging".'

'What!'

'Perhaps that wasn't the word.'

'That was the word all right. What a cheek! It's none of her business.'

'It's a perfectly normal question. She probably wanted to know if I was free tonight, that's all.'

'I don't believe I'm hearing this.'

'It's OK. I said I wasn't.'

'I should hope so!'

'Look, Justine, what you've got to understand is, you come from another millennium. As I said before. It's not surprising you're a bit old-fashioned. Nothing to be ashamed of.'

'Old-fashioned. Me!'

'You've come from a long way back.'

'I am not old-fashioned. I'm one of the most streetwise people I know, as a matter of fact.'

'Justine. We don't have streets any more.'

'It's an expression!'

'Sure. Anything you say.' He put an arm round me. 'How about that shopping?'

I shook his arm off. He wasn't going to get round me that easily. 'I haven't got any money.'

'That's not a problem.'

'I'm not having you buying me stuff.'

'I love it when you look cross like that,' he said.

'Huh.'

'Your lips go all pouty.'

He was giving me one of his hurt dog looks.

'Do they?'

'Mmmmm.'

'Are we going back to the mall?'

(OK. So he'd got round me. Look, the guy had offered to take me shopping, hadn't he?)

'Uh-uh. Not for the retro stuff. There's a market further down. They've got brilliant vintage clothing. It's cryonic.'

'Cryonic?'

'As in cool.'

'Oh, chilled.'

'We'll have to go down a few k, though.'

Los side-tracked off the main walkway and branched off crosswise into a kind of see-through tunnel and on to a conveyor which seemed unnervingly to be suspended in midair. This conveyor led us out to an elevator shaft. With a hiss of compressed air, a circular elevator, or 'verticator', as Los called it, docked.

'After you,' said Los.

As I climbed in, it wobbled unnervingly.

'Are you sure this thing is safe?'

'It's pneumatic, G-powered, totally fail-safe.'

The 'verticator' was one of those transparent external jobs designed to give even people who are fairly laid-back about heights a severe attack of the willies.

'A few k?' I swallowed. 'K as in kilometres?'

'That's right. Don't look so freaked out.'

'But I *am* freaked out. Where the hell are we?'

'Level 7777. Look out and you'll see. It's a really clear day.'

My knees had gone to jelly. And the glass, or whatever it was, was so clear it was hard to believe it was there.

I looked out and was rewarded by an attack of Fourth Millennium-strength vertigo.

'Oh my GOD!'

We were kilometres and kilometres above what any sane or normal person would call 'the ground' – i.e. nice solid, dependable planet Earth. We were above the height of Everest. Above the cloud line. We were above the height that jumbo jets fly. Below us, I could see the funny little Father Christmas shape of Britain, with the lumpy bit of Scotland sitting on top like a sack on his shoulder.

'Yeah, mind-blowing, isn't it? Welcome to Upside.'

'Upside?'

6

Upside. OK, I'll fill you in. Our journey down took a good ten minutes, during which time Los gave me the low-down on all this Upside–Downside business. It seemed a lot had changed since our time.

Apparently it all started with a big building boom mid-Third Millennium. There was this massive kudos thing about how high you lived – kind of the ultimate in our present day celebs trying to out-penthouse each other. The smartest addresses were over the thousandth floor and above. So naturally, these cool 'upper'-class people wanted to link up so that they could drop in on one another without all the drag of going down to where the plebs lived at the bottom. So they started building overpasses and linkways to join up their classy locations and these got higher and higher. And ended up – well, Los didn't put it quite like this, but cutting all the technocrap – basically 'Upside' was like a giant ring donut going right the way round the globe at a height of approximately 60k. And this whole donut thing was propped up by massively tall towers. We were going down the side of one right now at a speed of . . .

'A speed of what?

'Around 250 k.p.h.,' said Los.

'But we're not even moving!'

'Yes we are. We're at max. We're in free-fall.'

'!!!!'

'It's OK. We slow up some before we get to the bottom.'

'We'd better slow up lots.'

'There's plenty of time. We're still at 40k. That accounts for the Lo-G.'

'Lo-G. As in Low-Gravity?'

He nodded. I felt rather pleased with myself. I'd soon get the hang of all this scientific stuff. No sweat.

I leaned against the handrail and faced him. Our eyes met. He smiled and leaned forwards and brushed my hair out of my eyes.

Encouragement!

I moved a little closer. 'I couldn't believe it when I got your e-mail,' I said.

'I couldn't believe it when I got yours.'

'Really?'

'Yeah, well, I thought it was about time we met up.'

'So did I.'

'You know something, Justine? You're not like the girls up here.'

'Aren't I?'

'Uh-uh.'

'How do you mean?' I asked, preparing for a nice dose of flattery.

'For a start, you've got those little flecky things on your nose.'

(Oh grrrreat! Bonus. He'd noticed my freckles.)

'We don't have those here,' he said.

'No, I don't suppose you do,' I said flatly.

'No, I mean it. I really like them. They make you . . .' He paused, as if trying to find the right word. 'Different.'

I spent the next thirty seconds trying to work out if the word 'different' qualified as a compliment. *'Different?'* I prompted.

'Yeah. The girls here are all so, you-know, samey,' he continued. 'But you're something else.'

(I reckoned I could live with 'samey' if it meant looking like the locals but Los did seem curiously underawed by them.)

'Am I?' I said. I could feel a smile forming in spite of myself.

Los nodded. 'That's what I liked about your time. Way back in pre-history. I mean, everyone was different. You had all those weirdo kinds of people living together in those cute little baked clay dwellings . . .'

'Houses.'

'Yeah, and conveying themselves round in those cryonic self-drive people pods. And cooking stuff in pots on flames.'

Irritatingly, Los's concentration seemed to have slipped from me. His eyes had gone kind of distant. And his description of our time was making us sound like some backward hobbity kind of race I really didn't want to be associated with. I shifted his attention back to the here and now.

'But I really like it *here*. It's brilliant. It's really cool.'

'Do you?' He sounded genuinely surprised.

'Yes, it's all so absolutely mind-blowing. I mean, look at it!'

We'd just pierced a cloud bank. The low evening sun was turning the land below the delicious colour of freshly made white toast.

But Los wasn't looking at the view, he was staring at me. 'You look great in this light,' he said.

'Do I?' I said, my voice wavering. I could feel the threat of an agonising blush beginning to creep up my neck. Yes, sure enough, it was taking possession. It reached my face. I could feel my cheeks burning. And he'd noticed. (Thank you, body – I won't forget you for this.)

'How do you do that?' he asked.

'Do what?'

'You've gone a different colour.'

'No I haven't.'

'Positive. You have. Girls don't do that here.'

(What do you know? Another giant leap forward for mankind. They'd bred out blushing.)

To my intense mortification, he kept on staring. 'It's incredible. It's beautiful,' he said.

He moved in closer. I got a yummy whiff of his aftershave as his lips homed in on mine . . . (OK. Stop right there, body. Remember rule number one: treat 'em mean, keep 'em keen.)

With tremendous self-restraint, I took a step back. Or, rather, tried to. Something very strange had happened to my feet. I felt as if my mules had been glued to the floor. With a ginormous effort I managed to wrench one foot off and swing round to face away from him, removing my lips from their current temptation.

'What's wrong?' asked Los.

'My feet seem to have got stuck to the floor.'

He grinned. 'That's the G kicking in. Must be getting there.' He bent down and adjusted the tabs on his moon boots and showed me how to change the setting on my mules.

We'd arrived at our destination.

I'd been dreading that stomach-in-your-ears lurch when we stopped but I hadn't even felt us slowing down. With a gentle clunk, the verticator had docked. Silently the doors slid open.

We emerged into a gloomy steel corridor. I could tell at first glance that everything on this level dated back to an earlier era. There was more steel and concrete, less of this bouncy, see-thru stuff. And unlike up above, the light was a dim kind of greenish phosphorescence that made your skin tone look as if you'd been brought back from the dead.

There were no conveyors on this level either, just a tangled maze of footpaths running through steely corridors. Up above, it had all been so clean, so shiny, as litter-free as Switzerland. But down on this level there were signs of wear and tear. Nothing like dirt exactly but abrasions and worn patches as if these walkways had been used for centuries. I could even see places where graffiti had once been. They'd tried to erase it, but you could still make out the bulging outlines of centuries of tags.

There was one in particular. A shady outline that was somehow familiar. I stopped to get a better look. It was the word **LOVE** in four plain upright capitals with a big full stop after it.

'Hey, there's your tag!' I exclaimed.

Almost before the words had left my lips Los clapped a hand over my mouth. 'SSSSSH!' he warned.

'What's wrong?' I asked when I'd shaken myself free.

It was the name of his band: Lords Of Virtual Existence. Weirdo name but it was a pretty cool band.

Los walked a few steps forward and looked from left to right. When he'd ascertained that we were alone he said, 'Don't mention the band. They're Cyberians. We'll get lynched.'

'Cyberians? Lynched? What for?'

I'd come across the Cyberians before, in my time. They wore weird clothes, all black and silver. Dyed their hair an odd blue colour. Played a load of retro music.

'They seemed pretty harmless to me,' I said.

'They're a Downside cult,' said Los.

'So? What are they into? Ritual torture, human sacrifice?'

'No. Nothing like that. It's the stuff they sing. It's been banned.'

'What, old-time ballads? You're joking.'

'No, I'm serious. I'm not meant to meet up with them. The other members of the band. They're Downsiders.'

'What's wrong with that?'

'Downsiders and Upsiders, we're not allowed to mix.'

'Why not?'

We were approaching an intersection.

Los hushed me again. 'Watch out,' he warned and pushed me back against the wall. A group of guys built like baseball players zoomed across our path at around 100 k.p.h. At first glimpse I thought they were on rollerblades, but as they sped away I could see they were more like hoverblades, they didn't actually touch the ground. The guys had come and gone so silently, the shock took my breath away.

'Who were they?'

'RP squad. We'd better try and warn them.'

'Warn who? What's an RP squad?'

'Cops. They're out to catch Downsiders who've come up here to trade stuff.'

Los had broken into a run.

As he turned another corner we came face to face with a guy who had made a kind of ramshackle table out of slabs of polystyrene packaging. He was thin faced, his cheeks showing bonily through his skin, and his nose had a bend in it as if it had been broken somewhere down the line. On his tabletop he had a pathetic assortment of what looked like old straps and shoelaces, bits of string and a couple of ancient perished elastic bands.

His was first in a line of similar makeshift stalls. Most of the traders looked as if they were selling stuff you would've rejected for a jumble sale.

'RPs. Watch out, mate!' hissed Los.

The guy didn't need telling twice, he was already bundling up his merchandise. The message passed like magic down the line and within seconds a transformation had taken place. The stalls had disappeared and the walkway was lined with a workforce intent on their job – polishing the walls and floors.

There was an almost imperceptible hiss as the squad of RPs slid into view once more and slowed down as they passed the workers. Not an eye was cast in their direction.

One of the RPs stopped opposite Los and stared hard into his eyes. You could tell these cops were Upsiders by their build – brilliant-looking guys with Action Man square jaws and perfect pecs bulging under their gleaming armoured jackets. The one who was staring so hard at Los looked a bit like Arnold Schwarzenegger – but better.

'You wanna update your ID,' he said roughly, then he gestured to me: 'How long you got her for?'

'Oh, just the weekend,' I said with a smile.

The RP raised an eyebrow and leered. 'Well, have a good time,' he said and skimmed off to join the rest of the crew.

'What was all that about?' I asked.

'Everyone thinks you're a Simchick – it's the suit,' said Los.

His voice was interrupted by an ear-piercing whistle. Obviously this was the all-clear, because out came the bundles and crates, and the shabby line of stalls started to take shape again.

Los made his way along the line with a look of concentration on his face.

'Where did they get all this stuff?' I asked.

'They've been fossicking.'

'Fossicking?'

'They've dug it up Downside. Been scavenging in landfill sites.'

'Gross!'

'You gotta keep your eyes open. Find some genuine archaeological artifacts sometimes. Once heard of a guy who picked up an Amstrad.'

'A word processor?'

'Yeah well, you could call it that. He even got it to work after a fashion.'

I tagged along behind Los. Most of the stuff was electronics hardware. Looked like the bits the engineer left behind when he serviced Mummy's dishwasher. But as we rounded a corner I found there were clothes too. At least, I think they were clothes.

Some of these were actually in an almost wearable condition. It seemed that over the last millennium every style statement from Gap to Gucci had had its day – from totally shameless see-thru body-modelling, to robes so long and thick and all-encompassing you could have camped an average family inside. Skirts had been any length, so not much had changed there. I won't bore you with the trouser shapes, there are only so many variations you can play on those and I reckon we've had all of them in the past six months.

I trailed along, picking up things and rejecting them. You know how you do in totally gross shops? Like when you're taken shopping by your mother. Eventually you get so starved of style you totally lose your eye and latch on to some ghastly mistake that hangs in your wardrobe *forever*, taunting you.

But wait a minute – hang on. It was hardly worn at all and it was an original, definitely not a copy. I have an eye for these things.

'Oh-my-god. Look, it's a genuine Prada!' I said, holding up a handbag.

'What's a Prada?' asked Los.

'A real Prada handbag. I don't believe this!' It was, and it was the very latest – you know, the ones that have the big flat strap at the back.

'What's it *for*?'

'You put things in it so that you can carry them round.'

'How weird. What sort of things?'

'Like money and cashcards, except I guess you don't use them any more. And make-up which . . . erm, no one wears any more. And keys and tube passes and lighters and cigarettes . . .'

Los squeezed my arm and threw me a warning glance. But too late. We'd been overheard. People were eyeing me suspiciously.

'Did I say something?'

Los looked from side to side and whispered in my ear. *'Cigarettes* . . . Don't mention cigarettes . . . Not in present company.'

But it was too late. Already the word must've passed down the line. A shifty-looking guy wearing wrap-around shades emerged from between two stalls. With the merest gesture, he attracted Los's attention.

'Look what you've done. We'll never shake him off now.'

'What does he want?'

'He wants to supply us. They still grow the stuff down there.'

'What? Tobacco?'

'Shhhh! Look, put that bag thing down and concentrate. We're meant to be finding you something to wear, remember? Just ignore him and maybe he'll go away.'

'But this stuff is all so, like, pre-owned.'

'There's a really good stall up ahead. 2500 stuff. Pentecostal.'

Los headed off at speed and dodged between two stalls. I followed. It did the trick. We lost the guy.

'You mean, like, as in religion?' I gasped as I caught up with him.

'It's your sort of gear – it's black.'

'Just as long as it doesn't smell of garbage.'

But Los was right about the Pentecostal stuff. It was kind of DKNY understated. Our search came up with a chilled loose coat thing that fastened with a strip of digits you locked like a bicycle padlock.

'This is pretty cool,' I said.

'You want it?' asked Los. 'Don't look too interested.'

I nodded.

Los went over to the stallholder and held out a handful of shiny things which looked like shards of plastic. They stood and haggled for a while.

He came back, grinning, with the coat over his arm.

'Thanks.'

'You mean cheers?'

I nodded. 'Cheers. That was funny kind of money.'

Los shook his head. 'Not money. Downsiders don't use money. Not since they broke the banks, centuries back. But they'll trade for chips . . .'

He held out a couple to show me. They were little coloured shapes like the pieces of games you find in cheapo crackers.

'They don't look worth anything.'

'They're not to us. Obsolete. Stuff we trash all the time. But each holds a billion bytes of information. They'll do anything to get their hands on them.'

'Oh, computer stuff – bor-ring.'

'Not to them, they're not. We're meant to melt them down, but hey, what a waste, eh?'

Several Downsiders were eyeing the chips hungrily. Los shoved them back in his pocket.

71

'Come on, try it on,' he said, helping me on with the coat. He stood back and looked at the effect. 'Yeah, dressed like that I think you could pass for one of us.'

'An Upsider?'

He nodded.

'Oh right, cool.'

'Now you're clothed OK, I guess you could meet my moms.'

'You mean you've got more than one?'

'Haven't you?'

7

There were four of them: Mom, Grandmom, Great-grandmom and Great-great-grandmom. In fact, there was a fifth – 4GMom.

'Do you mean to say all of them live at your place?'

'Mom's place. Well, not all of them. Great-great-grandmom only virtually lives there. And 4GMom lives in a twilight home for the over 300s.'

We were on our way back upwards. And we'd got on to the subject of where I was going to spend the night. Back home, of course, if you stayed over with a boy, the sleeping arrangements would have been vetted or vetoed by parents. You know the scene – umpteen phone calls and loads of promises and reassurances from the host home. (Don't worry, they'll be on totally different floors and we're going to put on the burglar alarm, so there'll be no creeping around during the night.) But in 3001, I was outside parental control and I was starting to have a few of my own ideas about how I was going to spend the night.

'Anywhere'll do as long as we can be together,' I said.

'Oh, I don't live there,' he said.

'Where do you live?'

'Around.'

'So why can't I stay at your place?'

'Justine, listen to me,' he said. 'I don't have a place. Guys don't have places. What would I want a place for?'

'Somewhere to keep all your stuff for a start.'

'What stuff?'

'Like clothes and shoes and CDs and sports gear and letters and . . .' I thought lovingly of all the gear in my room. My wardrobe stuffed to bursting with the current season's impulse purchases. My shelves sagging under months of magazines. The collection of daft photo-booth photos of me and Franz and Max and Henry. And that precious carrier bag of letters, hidden well out of Mummy's way, on top of the wardrobe.

'What stuff?' insisted Los.

'Well everybody needs a home to keep their stuff in, don't they?'

He shook his head. 'Not any more.'

We'd arrived at our floor. We were heading back towards the midway concourse when Los came to a stop in front of a wall pock-marked with round porthole things. I watched as he made eye contact with a scanner.

'*Ident positive. What can I do for you*?' droned a mechanical voice.

'Change of footwear,' said Los.

'*Coming up.*'

There was a whizzing noise and almost instantly the nearest porthole slid open and revealed the typical messy interior of a boy's cupboard. There were several pairs of shabby moon boots like the ones he was wearing and a few empty simulator food cartons.

'You mean to say you live in a left luggage locker?'

'I don't live in there. I just keep my stuff in central storage. It's convenient. Means I can access anything, any place. Guys spend nights in VR mainly.'

'Virtual reality? Don't you ever sleep?'

'You do kind of. But not like old times. Why waste precious brain-time on nights of random search when you can choose what you want to dream?'

'What about girls?'

'Oh yeah, girls. We dream about girls lots.'

'No, what do girls do? Do they spend their nights in VR too?'

'Yeah, but they're into different stuff. Girls go in for role-play mainly. Like they'll choose a flick and edit themselves in. And girls do a lot of virtual partying.'

Partying! Role-play! Interesting. I could just see myself right now playing opposite Leonardo DiCaprio in *Titanic*. Or maybe standing in for Claire Danes in *Romeo and Juliet*, or maybe . . .

'You can really edit yourself into a film?'

'Sure. Trouble is, they feel so real people get addicted,' said Los.

'Like soap operas, my time,' I said in a superior way. (I suppressed the thought that the only real doubt I'd had about coming here was that I'd be missing the 'EastEnders' omnibus on Sunday.)

He leaned in through the porthole and selected a different pair of moon boots. As far as I could see they were identical to the ones he was wearing apart from the laces.

'Old favourites,' he said as he laced them up. 'Come on. We'd better get moving. Few minutes to virtual sunset.'

'You mean the sunlight's simulated?'

'Yes and no. Let's just say – it's recycled.'

I could hear a faint ringing in my ears. Gradually it was growing stronger until it rose to a high-pitched wail like a siren. The crowds were splitting apart and leaving the Mall.

Heading for side-turnings. The place had taken on a kind of rush-hour atmosphere.

'What's going on? Where's everyone going?'

'It's the curfew. We've gotta get you to Moms' place.'

'But it's Friday night!'

'So? What difference does that make?'

'Don't you meet up in pubs and clubs and stuff?'

'Not Upside. Not after curfew? But there's plenty to do in virtual.'

This was a blow. I'd been looking forward to a night out on the town. I hadn't come all this way to spend the future's equivalent of an evening in front of the TV.

'Why's there a curfew. Is there a war on?'

'Not as such. But there's unrest. And they're always on the look-out for Downsiders trying to infiltrate, specially at night.'

'But that's awful. Don't you mind staying in?'

'Depends what you call "staying in".'

Los then started to update me on the current choice of in-home entertainment. Mind-blowing! No wonder no one minded the curfew. I mean, what guy would want to stand around with half a lager in his hand doing lame things like watching girls dancing together, when he could spend the night shooting the virtual Niagara or playing Intergalactic Gladiators?

The crowds were thinning fast and Los had picked up speed. I was having trouble keeping up with him. Things might have moved on a bit in this millennium but my Lo-G mules had started rubbing a truly old-fashioned blister on my foot.

'How much further is it?'

'Too far. We'll take a G-pod.'

Now this was more like the kind of stuff I'd expected. A G-pod – didn't that have a cute futuristic ring to it?

Los had paused beside a brightly-lit yellow pole. Looked like a telegraph pole but kind of plasticky. He was being really irritating. He was just standing there, gazing into space. Why didn't he get a move-on? My feet were killing me.

'What are you doing?'

'Calling one up.'

'No you're not. You're not doing anything.'

'Yes I am. But all the lines are busy. It's peak time.'

'You mean you can just "dream" one up?'

'Er . . . kind of. Yes.'

I gave up at that point. I just slumped against the pole. God my feet hurt. And this suit was so-oo tight. We waited an age. It seemed that G-pods were about as predictable as number twenty-two buses.

Los frowned with concentration.

'What's happening now?'

'One's approaching. Watch out!'

At that point a little yellow vehicle, kind of the shape of a jellybean, whizzed into view overhead. I stepped aside as it homed to the pole then slid down and split open like a double pram. It was all wibbly-wobbly like an empty Babybel shell with two moulded seats inside. Frankly, I'd expected something rather more hi-tech.

'This is a G-pod?'

'Positive, climb in,' said Los.

I sank into one of the seats. Instantly the pod snapped closed, slid up the pole and zoomed off.

Within seconds we were swooping through the malls at a height of around fifty metres and a quite improbable speed. From inside, the pod looked totally transparent. It was the nearest thing you could imagine to a magic carpet ride. Which happens, you might know, to be my all-time favourite fantasy. But not at this speed, please!

'Oh-my-god! Oh-my-GOD! This is insane. What if we hit something?'

'We can't. It's pre-programmed. Look, if you're scared why don't you come over my side?'

I cast a glance at him under my lashes. He was so-oo gorgeous. With enormous strength of mind, I resisted.

He leaned back in his seat and grinned at me. 'What's wrong?'

'Nothing.'

'Come over here, then.'

I frowned at him. 'Haven't you got enough girlfriends already?'

'Always room for one more.'

'I can't believe I'm hearing this! I've come all this way and you just treat me like . . .' I paused for breath.

'A princess. Come on. I met you, didn't I? Took you shopping. Laid on a cool romantic meal – with flowers . . .'

'A flower. And that was a hologram . . .'

'Don't be like that.'

'Like what?'

'Grouchy.'

'I am *not* grouchy.'

I stared out of the window. I didn't want to admit it, but it wasn't the meal or the flowers or the shopping . . . It was him I wanted. And I wanted all of him. And all to myself. Not some measly little share of him with umpteen other girls.

He was looking at me again with that hurt dog look of his. Despite myself, I could feel my resistance crumbling. Maybe those other girls were just friends after all (admittedly – close friends). And he *had* been trying to please me (in his own way). I mean, what boy would give you flowers (OK – flower), and a meal (even if it was fast food) and take you shopping (in a market, but still . . .)? And buy you stuff (even if it was second-hand) . . . I hugged the coat closer around me and sank deeper into my seat. He smiled at me and patted the seat beside him.

Why was I being such a pain?

There wasn't really room for two on his side. I had to squeeze in ever so close. So, moving the relationship forward a notch, or even maybe two notches was, quite frankly, inevitable.

Our lips met.

Below us the lights of the mall sped by in a dizzying panorama. Above us, other G-pods swept silently through the air. It was like the biggest and the best fairground ride in the universe. All the thrills of a big dipper without the downside of leaving your stomach behind. On my personal Richter scale of ground-moving moments, this went right off the dial. And that was just the kiss.

'I'm really glad you made it up here,' said Los as we broke apart.

'So am I. I never thought you'd ask.'

'It was your e-mail. It made me realise how much you'd changed.'

'Did it?' I swallowed. (The thought of that e-mail still gave me a mega-cringe. Some of it even rhymed. But still, boys, you know, they're hardly connoisseurs, are they?)

I gazed out – blissfully – over the city. The lights were coming on, reflecting like a million stars on the endless gleaming surfaces of transpaflor. Beyond them, the evening sky was darkening to a fathomless indigo . . .

Just for the record, I'd like to state here and now that this was the very best moment of my life. (Even if everything goes downhill from now on. As it most probably will. I will at least be able to say to my children and grandchildren and the way things are going, great and great-greats too – that I have truly lived. Here I was, beside the man of my dreams, airborne in the most breathtaking city ever, with his arms locked round me. And he was taking me to meet his family. Sigh! Surely this must really and truly be LOVE?)

I was so glowing with the moment that I hardly noticed our pod slowing down. It came to a standstill hovering over a kind of vertical tunnel which disappeared into the top of one the buildings. Suddenly, with a kind of 'gloop', the pod was swallowed whole with us inside.

'What's happened?'

'We're docking,' said Los, and sure enough the pod popped open, tipped sideways and deposited us gently on to a little round, totally transparent balcony. 'This is Mom's place.'

8

Los was busy making eye contact with the Fourth Millennium equivalent of a doorbell. He was fussing about the fact that the scanner wouldn't recognise him – breathing on it and rubbing it with his sleeve. Which gave me useful time to look around.

So this was where he came from. A boy's home – primary source material in that vital information-gathering process. You can learn so much about a guy from his 'roots'. A first glance confirmed that it was all incredibly hi-tech, shiny-clean and reassuringly expensive-looking. Apart, that is, from a rather worrying artificial plant in a hideous blue plastic pot which had a mock-Grecian frieze running round it.

'Mom collects antiques,' said Los, pointing at the pot. 'That's Wedgewood.'

'Oh yeah, sure. My mother's got some of that too,' I said. 'Kind of.'

But Los wasn't listening. He'd resorted to thumping the scanner with his fist and kicking the door.

I brushed my hair out of my eyes. It's always a bit nerve-racking going to a guy's home for the first time. I mean, you can meet a boy and he seems perfectly normal. Then, when he takes you home, you find out the ghastly truth. Like his folks have seriously dodgy taste in carpets and they eat high tea at the most odd hour and give you absolutely nothing more till breakfast. And other people's bathrooms always smell weird, don't they?

Eventually one of those disembodied female computer voices responded in a rather slurred way: '*Welcome to the Angeles' multifunctional domestic unit. Protocol established. Stand by to ent. . . eeerrrrrr.*'

This was followed by the kind of crashing sound that a computer makes when the system goes down.

'Who's there?' Another voice came from inside. Sounding faint and very far away.

'It's me!' shouted Los.

'Hold it there. I'm coming,' the voice continued, gradually growing stronger. 'Whole system's on the blink again. Keeps crashing. All goes down. Everything's on manual . . .'

There was a slow grinding noise and the door was wound back a crack.

A small face, with the taut look of skin that's been stretched to its outer limits, was peering through.

'It's me, Gran,' said Los.

She peered at me. 'Who's that with you?'

'This is Justine. You know, the one I told you about?'

'Oh! Your little friend? From the past?'

'Positive,' said Los. 'Is Mom in?'

'G'day, m'dear.' Los's grandmom opened the door wider. 'S'glad to meet you.'

She was wearing a stretch all-in-one like a blown-up version of a Babygro. If you'd added a wibbly bit on top she would've looked exactly like a Tellytubby. The suit finished in suitable granny-ish fluffy pink slippersox which made an odd sort of crunching noise as she took a step towards me.

'How do you do?' I said, holding out a hand.

82

'Oh isn't that cute? Just like those old-time flix. G'day, m'dear.'

She struck my palm with a very strong and enthusiastic hi-five considering her age.

'Where's Mom?' asked Los.

He seemed nervous, which was understandable. Basically, I reckon introducing girls to your mother is a big kind of bonding issue. It's like the threshold into a guy's personal space. Face to face, female to female – the two of you are more than likely to see straight through his masculine facade. Naturally, most boys hesitate before letting you across.

'She's locked herself away in the Lo-G gym. Had such a scene this morning – discovered she'd gained a milligram – you know your mom,' his grandmom said, bustling on ahead of us. 'Now you come in and make yourself at home, m'dear . . .'

At home! I'll try to give you my first impression of Los's 'home'. You've heard of loft apartments? Well, multiply the average height of one by fifty. This was vertical living taken to the ridiculous. It was built in tiers like a cake-stand but with a hole going down through the middle. Currently, we were on the top tier looking down through the hole to umpteen floors below. I moved a step backwards.

'Take off those mules, m'dear, and make yourself comfortable.'

Grandmom was fussing about, finding me a pair of slippersox to fit. Los was already unlacing his boots and sliding his feet into similar ones which had weird fluffy soles like his gran's.

'Now these may be a bit big but at least they'll keep you rooted.'

Grandmom passed me a hideous pair of fluffy sox like her own, but with the current state of my feet I wasn't going to

83

complain. I slid them on and crunched across the floor after her. The carpet had a weird sort of texture that my feet kept sticking to. I felt as if I was walking in slow motion. Crunch, crunch, crunch, they went. Where had I heard that sound before? Fighting with the fastener of my duvet cover – Velcro?

'I'm afraid we'll have to go down manually,' she said as she disappeared down what looked horribly like a fireman's pole which led through the hole in the floor.

I stared after her. Vertical ladders absolutely freak me out. There was no way I was going down that pole.

'Isn't there a lift? Or stairs, maybe?' I asked Los.

He grinned. 'This is quicker. You'll get used to it. Go on.'

'Sorry. I'm staying up here.'

'Anything wrong?' Grandmom's head popped up through the floor like a gopher.

'Justine's never been down a G-pole before.'

'Oh, m'dear,' she tutted. 'I've seen those staircases they have in the flix. Lethal! You could kill yourself on one of those. Now, to my knowledge, no one's ever fallen down a G-pole.'

She disappeared from sight again as if to demonstrate how safe it was.

'Watch,' said Los, indicating a very small and inadequate step on the side of the pole. 'You put one foot here, hold on to the strap and you can go down as fast or as slowly as you like.' He slid after her.

'How do you come up again?' I asked suspiciously.

His head reappeared. 'Same way, just pull on the strap.'

'How does it work?'

'Lo-friction. It's no big deal,' he said, leaving me standing there. 'Look, either you try it or you stay up there. For good . . .' His voice echoed up from below.

I hesitated. It was a bit humiliating to be upstaged by someone's granny, so I gritted my teeth and climbed on.

Taking a deep breath and closing my eyes, I slid after them. Sure enough, I went down really slowly. I came level with Grandmom ten or so floors down. Los was nowhere to be seen. Further down still, I heard a familiar fridge-like clunk of a door. Huh! Raiding the fridge no doubt, if I know boys.

'Here you are, m'dear. I'll show you where you're sleeping and you can settle in.'

She paused at a kind of porthole with her head cocked on one side.

'*Proceed to select from options*,' came the electronic voice again. '*Office . . . living-room . . . bedroom . . .*'

'Bedroom,' said Grandmom and an entry fizzed open. 'There you are, you see? Talk to it nicely and it's all back working again.' She led me into a tiny room which was totally circular and completely bare.

'Umm. Silly question but – where's the bed?'

'Oh, you'll have to ask for it,' she said.

'Ask?'

'Like this: Bed!'

On cue a standard rectangular bed shape popped up out of the floor. She leaned over and unzipped the Velcro and there, sure enough, was a bed. Not exactly made up with traditional pillows and sheets but it looked comfortable enough.

She pulled out a bolster and gave it a shake and it inflated and fluffed up in her hands.

'There now. I'll leave you to yourself for a tick. If you want to call home, feel free.'

'Thanks. That would be nice.' (No, I wasn't daft enough to expect a phone.) I looked around for something that resembled a terminal. I'd promised to let Chuck know that I'd arrived safely. Not surprisingly, in all the excitement of meeting up with Los, I'd totally forgotten about him.

'Can I e-mail from somewhere?'

'Positive, no worries, just ask.'

'Terminal?'

A square of screen lit up on the wall.

'That's it. See, you've soon settled in.'

Momentarily it fizzed with static then faded out.

'Oh dear, we are having a day of it today, aren't we?' said Grandmom, thumping the wall with her fist.

The screen cleared and I spotted a little blinking icon with an e on it.

'Now look at that. Come good again. And Los says I'm hopeless with the gadgets.'

'Sorry, but where's the keyboard?'

'Keyboard?'

'Is it voice sensitive too?'

'Oh goodness me no, we may be a little backward but we're not that out of date. It can read your mind.'

I turned to the screen. Ooops!

'And to erase?' I asked.

'Start at the end and scan back.'

!SKCOLLOB

!skrow tI !dog-ym-hO

The screen blanked out again.

'Positive!' said Grandmom. 'You've already got the hang of it.'

'Thank you.'

'Cheers?'

'Yes, cheers,' I repeated and she turned and left the room.

The wall fizzed momentarily then re-formed behind her.

I went back to the screen. The little e-mail icon winked at me. I concentrated my attention on it. At that point a message came up in perfectly ordinary English:

Who do you wish to e-mail?

Now why couldn't computers back home communicate like that?

I racked my brain for Chuck's e-mail address. I reckon they design those addresses to be forgettable. But there was no need. The minute I thought of Chuck, a picture of him appeared on the screen, with two boxes beside it saying **Yes** or **No**. Brilliant! I thought 'Yes'. And the screen told me to **Go ahead**. This was just so civilised.

> **Hi! It's me, Justine. No worries. I've arrived!**
> **Errm. So much to tell you!!!!**
> **Errrm . . .**

No need to tell him every tiny detail, of course – the edited highlights of my day would do. At that point a picture of the Prada bag appeared on the screen. I erased it. Chuck hardly wanted to hear about a handbag, did he?

Despite myself, the bag reappeared.

It was such a nice bag. I gazed at it longingly. It was hardly worn at all. I was starting to have serious misgivings over not having insisted Los got it for me. I could picture myself back home, showing it off to Franz and Max and Henry . . .

> **Could you upload a handbag? I don't see why not. If I could be uploaded. That bag was real leather. Leather is only skin after all.**
> **And dead skin, unlike mine which was alive and had me inside it. Which must make it twice as difficult to upload.**
> **A handbag must be a cinch.**
> **Oh why didn't I go for it when I had the chance?**

I looked guiltily at the screen. It had faithfully taken down what I'd been thinking, word for word. Then I thought of the cutting comments Chuck would make about it. Prada! It would only serve to reinforce his view of me as a 'socially irresponsible consumer of luxury branded goods' – i.e. a truly dedicated shopaholic.

With determination I forced myself not to think any more about it. Chuck didn't want to hear about a handbag. He'd want to know something more scientific.

> Errrm.
> Guess what? I'm at least ten kilos lighter up here. And I haven't even had to cut out chocolate yet! Could be something to do with gravity, tho. Have to wear gross Lo-G mules to keep me rooted to the surface. Or pink Velcro slippers. Equally gross. Errm

Still not quite scientific enough for Chuck, so I added as an afterthought:

> P.S. Have not quite tracked down your equation yet.
> But I'm working on it.
> See ya
> :- x

All lies, I know! But I intended to ask Los about the equation the minute I next set eyes on him.

Another message flashed up: **Send?**

'Yes', I thought and the screen went blank.

So that was done. Not exactly a comprehensive account of life in this millennium. But no one expects volumes in an e-mail, do they?

I walked slowly round the room, taking in my surroundings, which didn't take long. Basically they consisted of four blank walls and a bed. No mags to flip through, no wardrobes to rake through, no drawers to snoop through. Not even a window to spoil the perfect symmetry of the space.

Where had Los disappeared to? Had he just dumped me here and gone off somewhere? That would be just my luck. Stuck in another time-span without a clue how anything worked. And dropping myself in it every time I opened my mouth. And over the weirdest things like mentioning his tag or even contemplating the very thought of a ciggie . . .

That's when I realised I had no idea how to get out. I started searching round the walls for some sort of button or switch or something. The walls were perfectly, uniformly flat. Panic attack!

But suddenly the entry fizzed open again and Los leaned in. He'd definitely been on a fridge raid. He was chewing. Had some kind of greenish mutant vegetable thing in his hand. By the look of it, the scientists had won their battle for genetically modified fruit'n'veg. It certainly didn't look like anything nature could possibly have dreamed up on its own.

'Want some?'

'No thanks. What is it?'

'No idea. Came out last week.'

He sat down on the bed. 'You OK in here?'

'Yes, fine.'

'Bed OK?'

'Think so.'

'Come and try it.' He smoothed a place beside him.

I sat down, a little way off, and bounced up and down a bit, you know how people do when they're trying out beds in shops.

'Want to connect now?' he asked with a casualness that totally took my breath away. (He even had his mouth full!)

'I've only just arrived!' I stammered like some idiot.

He shrugged. 'Suit yourself. But I'm stuck here now. It's after curfew.'

'Oh I'm really sorry if I've put you out,' I said.

Los frowned and got to his feet. He looked at me thoughtfully, still chewing on his vegetable. 'No worries. I'll spend the night in virtual if you like. I can bunk down anywhere.'

'Yes. I think that might be a better idea,' I said with dignity. Talk about taking me for granted!

He made as if to go and then paused at the wall. He turned back to face me. 'I think maybe I've upset you some way.'

'Well yes, actually. I don't expect much. But it might've been nice if you'd kind of worked up to what you just suggested.'

'Worked up? How?' He looked genuinely puzzled.

'Well you could've held my hand or gazed into my eyes or maybe just said I looked "nice" or something . . .'

He took another bite of his vegetable and chewed very slowly. 'Interesting,' he said. 'It's all that "love" stuff from back your time, isn't it?'

'Yes, I suppose you would call it that *love* stuff.' I was well and truly fuming by now.

Los looked at me assessingly. 'I think I better leave you to calm down some.'

'I think you had.'

And with that he left. The exit fizzed closed behind him.

I stared at the blank wall.

Well! Honestly! I thought. Men!

9

I sat, staring at the wall, wondering if what had just happened had just happened. I mean, I'd just thrown out the most drop-dead gorgeous man in the universe.

But he'd deserved it. Of course he'd deserved it. There was no way I was going to allow any guy to treat me like that.

Where had it all gone wrong?

I thought back over our relationship so far. Initial contact on arrival had definitely been positive. He hadn't been totally knocked out by my dress code, true, but we'd remedied that. He'd introduced me to friends as if we were an item. Then that girl had wanted classified personal information as if it was her god-given right. And she'd asked him if he was free tonight. Free tonight! When he was with *me*. What a cheek!

I lay on my back on the bed, staring at the ceiling. Sigh. I wished I could've brought Fred Bear with me. He was still at home, propped up on my pillow, with his one button eye dangling in that sympathetic way of his, missing me.

Double-sigh. Treble-sigh.

I know what my mother would've said: 'Well frankly, darling, when you'd made yourself so *available*, what did you expect?'

I know what Franz would've said: 'Jeez, Justine, you should be certified! If I'd been in your position . . .' (Yeah well, we all know what Franz would've done in *my* position.)

Henry would've told me that this was basically programmed male behaviour. Sad but true. Every male animal on the planet, from ant to zebra, had exactly the same attitude problem.

Max would've listened sympathetically and said: 'You did exactly the right thing. You went by your instincts. Only *you* know how you feel, Justine.'

And Chuck would've said: 'Get real. The guy's just trying it on. Tell him to G.A.L.'

And the thing is, every one of them would have been right.

I didn't know what to believe.

I wondered what Franz and Max and Henry would be doing right now. I was going to have to make up some pretty good stuff to impress them when I got back home.

Some Friday night this had turned out to be. Sniff.

Then I told myself firmly to get a grip. I needed to salvage what I could of my positive attitude, have a bath and maybe a hairwash and a good night's sleep. Then tomorrow I'd be back in action.

So where was the bathroom? Good question.

I got to my feet and started feeling my way round the walls. 'Bathroom?' I tried. Another door zapped open in the wall. No sweat! There was a further smaller room – a nice, reassuring bathroomy white – I stepped inside.

Like the bedroom had been, it was absolutely empty.

I cleared my throat. 'Loo?' I asked politely. Nothing happened. The word didn't seem to feature in the system's vocabulary.

'Lavatory?' I enquired, stepping up the pressure. Still nothing.

'Toilet? WC?' The room remained empty. 'Convenience?' I was starting to feel panicky now. 'Erm . . . Facilities? . . . Smallest room?' This was serious. I was fast running out of euphemisms.

'Oh what do you call it?' I pleaded.

On the word 'it' a very futuristic lavatory indeed appeared. I don't want to go into detail over the workings. The design of domestic appliances had moved forward in leaps and bounds. It took me quite some time to fathom out how it plugged into the suit. Basically, this is where Hoover met Whirlpool. It was quite an education.

Relieved, refreshed and recovering from this experience, I scanned the walls for signs of a tap.

'Shower?' I asked tentatively. Immediately water gushed out of the ceiling all over me. This was followed by these green nylon brush things whizzing round my body like a car-wash. I was soaped all over, up and into every little nook and cranny! Really! Soap was in my eyes and ears and all over my face. I opened my mouth to try to gasp 'Stop!' and got a mouthful.

And then, almost before I knew it, I was being sluiced down again and these hot air fans started up. Oh-my-god! I felt as if I was being boiled in the bag, literally. I felt myself sizzling inside the suit.

I climbed out of the bathroom and tried frantically to claw the beastly suit off. My Pentecostal coat had subsided in a sad little heap on the floor.

There was a knocking on the outer wall. My hair was dripping into my eyes and I was hot and wet and red as a beetroot. If that was Los again I'd kill him.

'Go away!' I yelled.

The entry fizzed open a crack. It was Grandmom.

'Oh, m'dear!' she said when she saw what a state I was in.

'Do you think you could unzip me or something?'

Grandmom shook her head and tutted as if this was a great joke. 'You can't unzip a simsuit. I've not taken to one myself. But loads of girls my age do. It sure does wonders for the figure.'

'Then how do I get out of it?'

'You don't. You'll need to be de-clothed professionally. But you can clothe as you wish on top. Positive.'

I lifted the dripping robe from the floor. Wet like that, it had turned into dolls' clothing. It reminded me of the mega-bucks floor-length crêpe dress I'd borrowed from Franz. I'd popped it in the wash before giving it back, and turned it into a tank top.

'Is there somewhere you could hang this up to dry?'

'Oh, m'dear,' she said. 'Didn't you zap the care code?'

'Is it totally trashed?'

'I'll do my optimum but can't predict outcome.'

'I've grown rather fond of it.'

'Is there anything else I can do for you?'

'Well, if it's not too much trouble, I'd love a cup of tea.'

'*Tea!*'

'With milk and sugar?'

Her voice dropped to a whisper. 'We don't allow "substances" in the house. Tea is available on scrip. but you have to be a reg. user.'

'What about coffee?'

She looked even more horrified. 'Same negative. *Caffeine,*' she whispered.

'Well, decaff would do at a pinch.'

It seemed her mind was made up on the hot drinks issue. So I settled for the most politically correct option I could think of: 'Do you think you could manage a glass of water?'

She went off and returned with my water in a sealed bottle

with the straw built into the top. The water was ice-cold but strangely flat-tasting. I had a horrible suspicion that, like everything else in the place, it must be recycled. There are some things it's better not even to think about.

'Thank you so much. I mean – cheers.'

'Cheers, m'dear. Have a good night.'

Naturally sleep was a total non-option. I tossed and turned and tried to get comfortable but the bed kept on moulding itself round me in a weird, disconcerting fashion. It was like sleeping in a jelly.

I hoped Los was having an equally miserable night. Serve him right. I reckoned maybe he'd gone off somewhere with those weirdo friends of his – the Cyberians. What were they up to? Probably something tediously political. Huh! Bor-ing.

And then I had a worse thought. What if he hadn't? What if he was surrounded by girls virtual partying? I bet he was, the two-timing creep – or three-timing or four-timing. He was probably with that girl right now – the one who'd asked if we were currently connecting.

I sat up on the bed.

She was so-oo sickeningly gorgeous. And she obviously had the hots for him. She'd be wrapped around him before you could say . . . anything. What boy could resist?

The tiniest flicker of envy, once ignited, started to lick round the borders of my mind. Before I could smother it, it had grown into a great raging fire of conviction.

He was probably getting off with her at this very moment. Or worse! Could one virtually 'do it'? Or didn't that count, like being a 'technical virgin'?

I stabbed at the pillow in fury. Men!

If only I had a book or something to take my mind off him.

I sat up again and asked the light to come on.

'**Book!**' I demanded.

'Book?' replied the wall, looking blank.

'Yes, book.'

The wall registered the electronic equivalent of amazement. '**Book???????**'

'**Book!**' I repeated. Surely, a simple enough request? A paperback would do. That couldn't be beyond it, could it?

There was a lot of flickering and flashing and the wall made a load of those funny gnittering noises that computers make when they're psyching themselves up to do something really difficult. And then a message came up.

Book downloading now.

'Thank you.'

But instead of a nicely dog-eared Mills & Boon appearing on the side-table, the screen leaped into life and that familiar tune filled the room. 'Oop-doop-doo I wanna be like yoo-hoo-hoo.'

The Jungle Book – oh, thanks a lot.

IO

Predictably enough, next morning I awoke trying to work out where on earth I was. Then I wondered what the time was. And then I remembered where I'd left my watch and it all came flooding back to me. Whatever the time might be, it was at least a thousand years later than I'd normally be getting up. So I decided I'd better get moving.

I stumbled into the bathroom and after several false attempts managed to access the basics in the hygiene and washing department. Once washed, a phial of what I took to be mouthwash appeared. I took a good slurp and experienced the most peculiar sensation in my mouth. It felt rather like having a mouthful of ants. I took a closer look at the phial. It was labelled:

Dental robots, please eject and re-use.

I could feel them delving right down between my teeth like an over-enthusiastic dental hygienist. Sure enough they made my gums bleed; I called up a mirror to inspect the damage.

Could I do anything as simple as look at my reflection? No way! The mirror decided to give me a total breakdown of the current status of every single bodily function in the medical dictionary:

Temperature: 37°C
Pulse rate: 70
Blood count: 13
Blood pressure: 110/70

I won't go into what it said further down. It got far too personal. Being faced with so much clinical information so early in the day was enough to bring on a serious attack of hypochondria.

In the hope that I was likely to live long enough for it to matter, I then spent a fruitless half an hour or so trying to do something with my hair. You'd think something so fundamentally crucial to human happiness as hair control would've moved on in a thousand years. Not a bit of it. In this type of air-conditioned environment, static causes havoc. Basically, I could now see why Sigourney Weaver had gone for a total skinhead in *Alien*.

I leaned forward to examine my skin. The mirror switched to close-up. Ghastly! My face looked like the surface of the moon – all my chickenpox scars etched on it like craters. Not a good start. Today of all days I needed the mirror to be on my side.

'Erase mirror,' I said with determination and it briefly glitched and faded out.

In the absence of hair control, make-up or even basic mirror support, I didn't have a lot to fall back on. Still, I couldn't stay in my room all day. I took a deep breath, wound my hair around itself and knotted it, then drew myself up to my full height.

Thinking positive thoughts with determination, I ventured out.

I paused outside my door, listening for sounds of life. Or smells maybe, of food cooking. I sniffed the air hopefully. Nothing. No bacon sizzling, no eggs frazzling, not so much as an acrid whiff of burnt toast. Maybe Mummy's prediction had come true and the entire human race had developed into a species of white goods browsers, whose only way of feeding was to lean into the fridge with the door swinging open and delve.

I crunched across to the G-pole and listened for signs of life from either above or below. There was a familiar hiccuping of laughter, music and applause coming from below – sounded like someone channel-zapping.

Sliding down one floor, I went to investigate. A room was in darkness with the door open. Inside, yet another granny was lying on a kind of futuristic *chaise longue*. As I peered in, the whole room lit up around us. It took me a second or so to realise that she was doing the equivalent of watching TV. Only this was in total surround sound and vision, and when I say total, I mean *total*. The screen went right over the ceiling and underneath my feet, then up again the other side. She was in the dead centre of a mind-blowing white-knuckle ride. I backed a few steps. The old dear's *chaise* thing was careering back and forth as if it wanted to throw her off. But it didn't seem to faze her one bit. She just sighed in a bored kind of way and tutted and zapped. Another visual came up of tea being poured into a cup.

'One lump or two?' asked a voice.

This was greeted with a squeal of horrified delight.

A concerned counsellor voice cut in, saying, 'Today, m'dears, we know better, don't we . . .'

She sighed and tutted and zapped again.

Down one more floor, I came face to face with an even older lady. She hadn't heard me. She was eating something from a bowl with a look of concentration on her face. Breakfast? This looked promising. Oh what I would give for a bowl of Coco Pops.

'Good morning,' I ventured.

She took no notice.

'Hello?'

Still no reaction. Maybe she was deaf. I took a step towards her and walked slap-bang into a wall. It took me a second or two to realise that this wall wasn't a wall at all, but a screen. It filled the entire ceiling-to-floor area and looked as real as real life, if not more real, if you know what I mean. Everything was etched in super high resolution.

As I watched, she looked up vaguely from her bowl and pointed a zapper at the screen. 'I'm clean outta sugar,' she announced.

I was just wondering if I ought to offer to get some when I was interrupted by Grandmom's voice talking over some kind of intercom: 'Remember, 3G-dear. You have to click the spoon icon for the no-cal sweetener . . .'

That's when I realised that the granny on the other side of the screen must be Great-great-grandmom, the one who 'virtually' lived with them.

I slid down another floor. Distinctly kitcheny sounds were emerging through a further wall. I approached warily this time. As I did so, that irritating disembodied voice spotted me and announced in a haughty tone: *'You are entering a food preparation area. Pause for total de-bacterialisation.'*

I felt myself being held in check as a rush of icy air whooshed over me. The room ahead was a kitchen all right. The entry was open just a crack. But everything inside was so hi-tech that nothing remotely suggesting food was on view.

I'd read about kitchens like these. They shopped for you, cooked for you, and in a really creepy way, their wastebins checked up on what you'd eaten and informed on you. So that the supermarket could sell you stuff before you even realised you were out of it. Dodgy, if you ask me. What if you kept chucking out stuff you didn't like? You'd get inundated.

I craned forward to get a better view. No doubt they had all these super-intelligent appliances which communicated with each other. You could imagine them, couldn't you? Having girly chats together – 'Oh, that's a nice magnet you've got on, fridge.' 'Oh, do you like it?'

The whoosh of cold air eased off and the voice announced: '*Process completed. You may now proceed.*'

The entry fizzed open wide enough for me to pass through.

Los was in there, perched on a spindly kind of bar stool and, as I'd predicted, digging into something. But not alone. He had the most drop-dead gorgeous girl with her arm round his shoulders. She was wearing some minimal body-skimming sportswear, hardly decent, and had a towel draped round her neck. Oh, this was getting really out of hand.

I stepped through the entry and stood there, outwardly calm, inwardly self-combusting.

'Hi,' I said.

The girl stretched up to her full height and crossed her arms. '*Who* is this?' she asked, as if she owned him.

'No, look, listen.' Los was on his feet now, saying apologetically to this imposter. 'I can explain everything.'

'Explain away,' said the girl. 'I'm listening.'

'Now wait a minute,' I said. 'I think I'm the one who's due an explanation. What's *she* doing here?'

'What am *I* doing here? I live here!' stormed the girl.

I paused. An awful thought had just struck me.

'Justine,' said Los. 'I'd like you to meet Mom.'

Oh this just wasn't fair. Boyfriends' mums weren't meant to look like this. They should be suitably greying and wrinkly. Tactfully overweight. Blokes' mums are intended for contrast. To show up how much younger and prettier and more switched on you are. They shouldn't be taller and slimmer and blonder and basically a babe like this one.

But 'this one' was currently giving me a very hostile look. And her eyes were resting in a most uncomfortable manner round about my chest level.

I suddenly became all too aware of my twin size 38Ds. I felt myself flushing scarlet. I hadn't felt this embarrassed since I bumped into Mr Wilkins, our IT teacher, on that topless beach at St Jean-Cap-Ferrat.

'Would you mind if my son and I had a moment *alone* together?' she said.

Los raised his eyebrows at me and I slunk out.

(This was not at all the kind of meeting I'd pictured. I mean, she wasn't exactly bringing out the album and cooing over Los's baby pictures with me, was she?)

I wouldn't say I was eavesdropping exactly, but I couldn't help overhearing the odd word:

'. . . I told you . . . ever to bring . . . here again.'

'But she's not a droid.'

'She's a droid if ever . . . one.'

'No I promise you . . .'

'Sometimes . . . wonder where I . . . wrong.'

'. . . not a droid.'

'Then . . . she, then?'

'. . . come from a long way . . .'

'She's not a . . .' This last word was lost in a clash of something being slammed on the worktop.

'No way!'

'I don't believe you.'

'Don't, then!'

'Los . . . I want her out of here . . .'

'Mo-om!'

'Now!'

I backed away from the entry. Usually, with effort, I get on really well with other people's mums. But something told me that calling her Mrs Angeles and buying her a pot plant and taking an in-depth interest in her ornaments wasn't going to solve this one.

Los burst out of the kitchen looking furious. 'Come on,' he said. 'We'd better make a move.'

He shot up the G-pole ahead of me. I followed.

On the floor above, Great-grandmom called out from her room for us to stop. Great-great-grandmom was banging on the screen with her spoon, complaining about all the fuss. Grandmom came popping up through the floor on the G-pole after us, demanding that Los should tell her what was going on.

The two of us paused for breath on the top floor.

'See why I don't live at home?' Los gasped as we made our escape.

That's the thing no one ever predicts about the future. They go on about the good bit. The fact that all the illnesses and ageing processes will have been conquered – and you're not going to sag and dry out and wrinkle like the standard olds of today. You're going to stay young and fit and live to an incredibly old age still looking presentable.

Nobody mentions the fact that so are your parents and their parents and their parents' parents and even their parents' parents' parents. Until everyone will have this incredible hierarchy of 'olds' – all of whom are bound to take a pathological interest in what you do and want to have their say in it.

11

We were back in a G-pod once again, heading back to the central concourse.

'Sorry about all that,' said Los.

'What was all the fuss about?' I asked.

'Oh it's just Mom being paranoid. Don't take any notice.'

He leaned over and took my hand and kind of toyed with it thoughtfully. My heart turned over with a thump. (Thank you, Mom! There's nothing like a healthy dose of parental opposition to move a relationship forward.)

'No, tell me. I'd like to understand,' I prompted.

'She thought you were a simchick.'

'Oh right, thanks a lot.'

'I tried to put her right. And then it got worse.'

'Worse?'

(Worse than being taken for a 3-D equivalent of a porno magazine?)

'Now she thinks you're a Downsider.'

'What's wrong with that?'

'I guess she's just prejudiced.'

'Against Downsiders? Why?'

Los looked uncomfortable and started fiddling with the

laces of his moon boots.

'You know how, in your time, your mum and dad wanted to give you the best start in life?'

'You mean like Startrite shoes, fixed brace, CD version of *Encyclopaedia Britannica* – all that stuff?'

'Yeah, kind of. Here the whole thing starts earlier.'

'Like playing classical music to the womb?'

He shook his head. 'Now we know what genes determine what, they can kind of plan how you'll turn out.'

'Oh boy, genes. That accounts for it.'

'Accounts for what?'

'Why you're all so simply, utterly and completely perfect.'

'Oh we're not perfect, negative, no way!'

'You're not?' (Looking at him now, with his blue eyes and hair all tousled like that, you could've fooled me.)

Los held out his hand for inspection. 'Just look at that.'

You know those little white flecks you get in your nails? He pointed out the minutest one on his index finger. It was so tiny I had to squeeze up my eyes to see it.

'I keep getting them. I blame my mom. Something wrong in the gene mix.'

I decided to humour him. 'Oh come on. What about your dad? It might be his fault?'

'Negative.'

'Where *is* your dad by the way?' (I'd have liked to have met him. Generally, I get on a lot better with boys' fathers.)

'That's the thing,' he said. 'We don't have dads any more.'

'Come off it. Everyone has to have a father somewhere.'

He shook his head. 'Negative. Not any more. Not Upside.'

'I don't believe you.'

'A free choice of fathers just messes genes up.'

I could see he had a point there. Basically, I blame Daddy entirely for the shape of my nose.

'No fathers at all?'

'Not unless you count the municipal gene pool.'

I stared out of the window while I got my mind around this one. Imagine a world without fathers. No one to remind you to switch off the lights. No one to go through the family itemised telephone bill with that look on their face. No one to have that miserly attitude to upping your dress allowance or handing out an advance.

And then I thought of the other side. No one to tap the barometer in the morning and say: 'Hmmm' the way Daddy did. No one to mow the lawn and set out the sunloungers for you. No one knowing what tyre pressure the car has or which hole the oil goes in. I supposed fathers had their uses.

'But don't you ever wonder about your dad?'

Los shook his head. 'It's not like that. They just take the best genes from all kinds of guys and blend them together.'

For a moment, as I stared at Los, I felt a rush of sympathy. Poor babe, fancy coming from a municipal gene pool? No wonder he was so 'mixed up'.

'I'd like to have a dad, though, like your time.'

'Really?'

'Yeah. And real brothers and sisters. And we'd all eat together and go off on vacations to the ocean and stuff.'

'You mean like a family?'

'Yeah.'

I thought back to the last disastrous family holiday we'd had. The never-ending battles with my sister Jemima over who'd brought sand into the bedroom and whose turn it was to be first in the shower. And as for eating together, Sunday lunch was basically the war zone where we sorted out the family feuds. Daddy only had to raise the carving knife for hostilities to break out.

'Families aren't all they're cracked up to be,' I commented.

'They still have them, you know. Downside.'

'They do?'

'Yeah. Nothing much has changed Downside. They're still really primitive. They still have couples and things. They still even get whad'ya call it? Yeah, 'married' sometimes.'

'I'm relieved to hear it.'

'You don't understand. Upside is where everyone wants to be. Downsiders are desperate to get up here. They'll do anything. Body moulding, implants, plastic surgery. But they always get found out and sent back. You see, however hard they try, they never look quite like us.'

'And your mom thinks I'm a Downsider. Thanks a lot.'

'There's nothing wrong with Downsiders.' He leaned forward and whispered in my ear conspiratorially: 'Downside – that's where it's all happening. That's where we all go. All the crowd. Saturday nights, it's down the tube to Downside.'

'What do you do down there?'

'Meet up with friends. Do some music maybe.'

'With the band – the Cyb . . .'

Los shot me a warning glance. 'Look, just don't mention them, OK? Not Upside.'

I nodded. 'It's Saturday *today*,' I said.

'Positive. Get you wired first so you can try out virtual,' he leaned closer still. 'Then, after curfew – I'll show you some *real life* Downside.'

'Wired? Is that really necessary?'

I didn't like the sound of it. Wired. Nasty, painful-sounding word. I'm a total physical coward, you see. I'm still the only one in the class who hasn't had their ears pierced. I couldn't find anyone willing to do it under a general anaesthetic.

We docked the pod in Central and took a conveyor through

to the Midway Concourse. All the way I was pestering Los about getting me a watch. I was really missing my Tag; I needed some way of telling the time.

He said not to worry, he'd fix it, he knew this cool place in the mall.

I looked around hopefully, expecting to see some kind of jewellery or watch shop. But there was something really weird about the shops. Now that I had time to take a closer look, I wasn't so sure if they *were* shops. Maybe they were just façades? It was difficult to tell. You'd scan down an arcade and just the act of looking set into motion giddying waves of electronic colour.

Wherever you looked, clashing logos leaped into life, sending a constant bombardment at your senses: GARB-AGE, POD-U-LIKE, GAME GRAN. They were using every trick in the designers' book to fight for attention: neon, strobes, animation, animatronics. You only had to stop for one moment and three-dimensional holograms detached themselves from the façades and approached you, trying to persuade you into a demo. Some started talking to me like the boy on the hoarding had. They were so real I kept on stopping and answering them.

'Come on,' said Los. 'We'll never get you wired if you keep lagging behind.'

'It seems so rude to just walk by.'

'Justine, they're sims. Ignore them.'

I trailed behind him. It was pretty hard to ignore some of the guys. How would you feel if you had the equivalent of male film stars, or supermodels as large as life and just as gorgeous giving you the eye and calling out to you to come over, just for a minute, and spend some time with them? I'm telling you, it gave window-shopping a whole new meaning.

One of them in particular was so convincing he seemed to

come out of the wall at me. I even had the impression he was tugging at my sleeve. Now this was truly amazing.

'You want cigarettes?' he asked in a half-whisper.

I was just about to walk by when I realised that he wasn't a sim at all. He was the guy whom we'd met at the market. The dodgy Downsider in the wrap-around shades.

Los hadn't noticed that I'd stopped. I was tempted to answer that I wouldn't say no to twenty Marlboro Lites if he had some going, but at that moment Los stopped and shot a glance over his shoulder, looking for me.

'Justine!' he said. He was back in a flash. He told the guy in no uncertain terms to get lost and took me by the arm and started marching me along.

'Do you realise what that stuff does to you?'

Honestly, this was worse than being lectured by Daddy. 'Err well, yes, but . . .'

'I thought you had Health Education back in your time?'

'Yes we do, but no one really takes any notice of . . .'

'Well you should,' he said. 'Look, Justine, you've got to realise. I'm saying this because I really care about you . . .'

'You do?' (Same words maybe. But this sounded totally different not coming from Daddy.)

'Positive.'

I slipped my arm through his. *'Positive?'*

(He'd said it. He cared about me. He really, really cared about me. I don't know about this millennium, but back my time, I reckon 'caring about' is male code for *love*.)

12

Los had paused at an entry. Above him a logo lit up in dazzling strobes: **Terminal Chic**.

I followed him inside. Weird store: no counters, no racks, no assistants, nothing to buy as far as I could make out. All I could see were a couple of cushy recliners on weird sort of plinths which reminded me threateningly of dental chairs. Los bounded into one and patted the other for me to climb in.

'Cryonic!' he said. 'They've got evil stuff here. Might even upgrade myself.'

'But where is everything? Can't I browse? Can't I choose?'

'Uh-uh, negative – nothing to look at. You'll see what I mean in a mo.'

I slumped into the other recliner. Some shopping trip this had turned out to be. Nothing to listen to. Nothing to try on. Nothing to test. Bor-ing.

A screen flashed to life about fifteen centimetres from my eyes. And a disembodied voice said: *'Boot up. Jack in. Crash out. Get into Terminal Chic.'*

I hissed at Los. 'All I really want is a watch. Doesn't have to be designer or anything. A cheapo digital will do.'

'Shhh!' he said. 'Sit still.'

'*Please place your order after the tone.*' *Beeep*!

'Initial brain port installation,' said Los and a load of options came up on a vid. I could tell by the way they were flashing and bleeping that Los was mentally selecting from them. He leaned over and winked at me. 'OK?'

'No. What's going to happen? What are you doing?'

'Just selecting the installation you want.'

'I don't want any kind of "installation".'

'I promise you, you won't feel a thing.'

At that moment this kind of clamp thing came round my head and I felt my ears being grasped by what felt like cold metal fingers. I cowered as, to my intense and utter horror, two huge kind of dental drills swung down from the ceiling and homed in on me.

I tried to scream 'No!' but my mouth had gone dry. The sound came out as a kind of squeak.

The drills went 'thunk' simultaneously and my ears sort of reverberated.

'All over,' said Los.

The clamp loosened from my head and I sat up.

Tentatively, I checked my ears. I could feel that two studs, like the ones Los was wearing, had been inserted in my earlobes. He was right, it hadn't hurt. My ears weren't even sore.

'Cool! Painless ear-piercing! But I wish I'd had a choice. Are these real gold? I'll sue if I get an infection.'

He shook his head. 'You won't. They're de-contam, anti-bac, pro-allergen, contra-oxyde and genetically perfectly matched to your DNA profile.'

He was climbing out of his seat.

'Is that all?'

'What did you expect?'

'Well, at the very least I wanted some way of telling the time.'

Los grinned. 'What's the time, Justine?'

'Two thirty-three and thirty-four seconds,' I said automatically. 'How do I know that?'

'You're wired,' he said with satisfaction.

'You sure?'

'Square root of 475?'

'Twenty one point seven-nine-four-four-nine-four-seven-one-seven-seven approximately.'

'Correct. Diameter of the Sun?'

'One million, three hundred and ninety thousand and nine point twenty-one kilometres. Why on earth would I want to know that?'

'I guess it just comes with the package.'

'Package?'

'Basic start-up infopack. Don't want to overload you.'

'You mean I know all this stuff because I'm wired?'

'Uh-huh.'

'What else do I know?'

'Loads.'

'I don't know if I like this. I feel kind of weird.'

'You'll soon get used to it. Come on.' He held out an arm to help me down from the recliner. 'Let's get going.'

I checked the ear-studs in the mirror, they were quite cool actually. 'Do I have to pay for these or what?'

'You already have.'

'I can't have? How?'

'Auto-debit, from your bank account, back your time.'

'But I only had £25.50 in my account.'

'Plus a thousand years' interest at a mean average of 3.25% APR,' said Los. 'Work it out.'

'One pound, nine-seven-nine-seven-nought-five-one times ten to the power of fifteen. Which is nearly two million billion pounds. The sum came out without even thinking about it. Bonus! Back home I was still trying to pass GCSE

Maths. Here, I'd become a numerical genius – a walking-talking calculator. I couldn't wait to tell Chuck.

We headed back out into the mall. But I was having trouble concentrating. Really, really odd thoughts kept flitting through my mind. Stuff that had never even occurred to me before. I had to slow down while I tried to think clearly.

'What is it now?'

'It's all this money stuff. I keep thinking about finance. Wondering if I'd be better in a savings option. Or a pension plan. Or whether I want a loan. It's weird.'

'You're getting Spam. Junk mail. Sorry, hasn't been vetoed yet. Stand still. Look to me. Concentrate. You see that little symbol flashing in the corner of your eye?'

'Oh my god. Yes!'

'Switch it to Off.'

'How?'

'Think Off.'

I did. 'It's gone!'

'You're getting the hang of it.'

'What did I do?'

'Alerted a kill file. That should edit out the junk. What are you getting now?'

'Another little symbol. Kind of like e-shaped.'

'You've got mail.'

'E-mail?'

'Yeah, open it.'

'Think Yes?'

He nodded.

'Where the **** are you? What's happened? What's all this about a handbag? I'm worried sick. CND

It was from Chuck.

'It's from someone back home. How did he get through?'

'You're wired. Your e-mail automatically gets redirected.'

'Over a *millennium*?'

'Whatever. Time makes no difference in cyberspace.'

'Boy! Chilled! You mean I can communicate with anyone back home?'

'As long as they're on e-mail.'

But I wasn't listening. I was already trying to e-mail Franz. Sure enough her picture appeared in the little box in the top right-hand corner of my optical field. Yes!

> Hi Franz
> Guess who I'm with!
> : X !
> There are things here to fry your brain!
> E-mail me back!
> J XXXX

And then I remembered that she was currently out of circulation stranded on a boat with her father, so I e-mailed Chuck instead. He appeared in the box looking as dweeby as ever, he even had his gross Earth Summit baseball cap on. S.A.D.

> Hi! It's me. Justine
> Everything's fine.

I paused for inspiration and then added:

> Still trying to track down your equation.
> Jx

'What equation?' asked Los.

'You were eavesdropping on my e-mail!'

'So?'

'That means . . .You were reading . . . my mind.'

'So?'

'I don't believe you. That's impossible!'

'No it's not.'

'OK, so what else am I thinking?'

He stood back and stared at me thoughtfully. I glared back. God – look at those pecs, he had such a fit body under that T-tank.

'Justine! You're mentally undressing me. Put my T-tank back on this minute.'

'Oh my god, you can! How?'

'You're on-line. I'm on-line. We're cross-posting.'

'But I can't read yours.'

'Positive – you can. Try.'

'I can't.'

'Just concentrate. Think of what I'm thinking.'

I tried.

A tiny picture of my face flashed up. Weird – like accidentally catching sight of yourself in a mirror.

'Oh-my-god. It's me!'

I looked quite cute actually. In fact, quite kissable at present. My reflection closed its eyes and the action zoomed in on the lips. So he wanted to kiss me.

'Oh-my-god, I can! At least I think I can . . .'

I half closed my eyes and leaned towards him. And then he changed his mind. Uh-huh, he was thinking. Remember last night? My turn to play hard to get this time.

Oh pants, I thought.

He laughed and put an arm round me. 'So who was that guy you were e-mailing?'

'Just a friend.'

'What's he like?'

'Errm, well . . .'

With a tremendous effort, I managed not to think of Chuck and thought of David Beckham instead.

'Ah. . . huh,' said Los with a frown. 'And you're really close friends with this guy?'

'Yes, very close indeed.'

'Uh, huh,' he said again. He took his arm away and thrust his hands in his pockets. He looked at me under his eyelashes. (Frankly, David Beckham was rubbish compared with him.)

'Is that the guy you were staying over with? The one you told me about in your e-mail?'

'Which e-mail?'

'You only sent me one.'

I suddenly had an awful thought. Which one? 'What did it say?'

'Can't remember exactly. I can access it and check if you like.'

Suddenly my e-mail flashed up in his mind.

> Hiya!
>
> How's it all going?
>
> Ignore everything in my last e-mail. Some ghastly mix-up with my English homework. Aren't those romantic poets pa-the-tic? Talking of romance, I'm taking Franz up on that bet of hers. To see who can get off with the most guys by Christmas. Currently having the coolest time with bloke number seventeen.
>
> If you wanna get in contact I'll be staying over at his place mainly at http://ourworld.compuserve.com/webwonderstud/cnd

'Oh my GOD!'

How could I be such an airbrain? I'd only said it to make him jealous. And he'd obviously believed every word of it. Oh, why do men have to be so *literal*?

I walked along beside him, kicking myself for being so truly idiotic and immature as to write that e-mail. Then cursing Daddy's Apple Mac for not failing to send it. Typical!

This was bad news. No wonder he'd tried to make a move on me last night. He obviously thought I was anyone's. And I wasn't. I mean, I never had been *anyone*'s. What could I do to put him right? Something told me the time had come, as the good old problem pages tell you, to 'talk things through with the guy'.

I took a deep breath. They made it sound so easy, didn't they? Like you could just casually chat to a male about sex, like you were discussing your latest buy in Our Price or what was in-store at the Virgin Chelsea.

'About that e-mail . . .' I started.

He put an arm around me. 'Mmmmm?'

(This was really difficult.)

'Well, I didn't really mean . . . What I mean is . . . I really didn't mean I was actually going to get . . .' I paused.

'Going to get what?'

'Well it was more of a kind of challenge really, saying I was going to get off with . . .'

His eyes had gone all kind of distant.

That's when I realised he wasn't even listening to me. With determination I accessed his mind. He was cross-posting with a couple of the guys we'd met in the mall. I could see pix of them both. One was Rio the guy in the potato sack. And the other was the blond dreadlocks guy, who'd called himself Tyrone. They kept on interrupting each other. The three of them were having a heated discussion about what game they were going to play this afternoon. Men! Typical!

That's the thing they don't tell you about communications. They go on about how absolutely brilliant it is to be in touch with everyone, everywhere, all the time. What they don't tell you is that everyone you want to be in touch with is highly likely to be in touch with everyone else. Which means, of course, that you can't get through to the person you're currently with.

Los had started walking again in a purposeful way. I caught up with him.

'Could you please give *me* a little attention?'

'Sorry. Where were we?'

I took a deep breath. 'I was just trying to explain that I wasn't really intending to get off with all those guys.'

'Oh? Why not?'

'Why *not*? Because I'm not that sort of girl, that's all.'

'What sort of girl is that?'

'The sort of girl who gets off with lots of guys,' I said, rolling my eyes in exasperation. (Either he was sending me up or he was being incredibly dense.)

'So why did you tell me you were?'

'OK. I admit it. I wanted to make you jealous.'

He looked genuinely confused. 'Jealous?'

'Yes. You see, I reckoned that you had all these girls after you . . .'

'And you didn't like that?'

'No, of course not.'

'Isn't that a bit selfish?'

'No! It's perfectly natural. I wanted you all to myself.'

'Justine. Just let me try to get my mind round this one. You told me, incorrectly, that you were "getting off" with loads of guys. Because you thought that this piece of information would make me want to stop "getting off" with loads of girls. Is that right?'

'Yes. Well. Kind of.'

He'd stopped again. He took hold of me by both shoulders and looked into my face. 'Justine. Think about it.'

I could feel myself going scarlet under his gaze. 'Well, I guess it is a bit crazy when you put it like that.'

'A bit crazy!' He was grinning at me. 'You're going that cryonic pink colour again.'

I broke away from him. 'I am *not*.'

It was at that point that Tyrone's thoughts cut in again. 'Hey, man. Can't wait all day. Bring that dumb-brain female with you.'

'I am not a dumb-brain!'

'No. Just a thousand years out of date, that's all. It's understandable.'

'And there's no need to be so condescending.'

'Come on,' said Los. 'Come and update yourself, then. Get into some virtual. We gotta catch up with the guys.'

13

Tyrone and Rio had arranged to meet up with Los at something called the Air-o-drome on level 93,996. This was great, a team outing, just when I thought I was going to get Los all to myself for a while.

As the verticator rose, Los was busy on-line with them, planning my 'afternoon's entertainment'.

I was listening in with only half an ear; they were going through the choice of 'evil' games. I stared out at the view. The world below us was getting further and further away. I could now see the whole of Britain and the great big dinosaur head of Scandinavia looking as if it was about to swallow Denmark.

'Yeah, could take her on a Tourisk Tour – like Atlantis, for instance, but girls never like getting wet. Didn't you get drowned in that last time? Transmutation – that's kinda weird but not bad if you're really into animals. Xdream Sportz – now that could be interesting . . .'

He turned to me. 'Justine, you fancy trying some sportz?'

I was just about to answer in the negative when I remembered yet another gem of problem page advice: 'Find activities that will allow you to develop similar interests . . . like dancing, saving the environment or sports . . .'

'What sort of sports?' I asked.

'Xdream Sportz – everything you've ever wanted to do and never dared.'

'Like?'

'Er . . . Hi-wire salsa. Sub-ice-cap scuba . . .'

'How about something a bit less energetic?'

'How about flying? We could take you on a Phantasy Flite.'

Knowing boys, this was likely to be just as scary.

'How big is the plane?' I asked suspiciously.

Los laughed and shook his head. 'Don't let it worry you. It's only virtual.'

We met up with the others in the locker room of the Air-o-drome. Typically, as soon as they set eyes on each other the guys got their heads together talking boy-stuff as if I'd become part of the decor.

'Guess they didn't have Sportz back her time,' said Tyrone, glancing at me over his shoulder.

'Yes they did,' I cut in.

'Like what?'

'Er, like football for instance.'

'Footwhat?'

'Football. You know, two teams of guys kicking a ball around.'

'Grown-up guys? What did they do that for?' asked Rio.

'Well, it's a game.' I paused, my knowledge of football was sketchy. 'They played in things called leagues.'

'A game. A game in which grown men just kicked a ball around? You're kidding,' said Rio.

'Nah, nah,' said Tyrone. 'I've seen old vidz of it. It was a kind of religion back her time. Haven't you heard of Soccah? They went into trances. Thousands of them, chanting. Mass hysteria, grown men crying. All that kinda stuff.'

'Primitive,' said Rio, shaking his head.

We joined a queue of other flyers getting fitted out and I was handed a flight pack.

'What is it, a parachute?' I asked.

The guys exchanged 'isn't-she-a-dweeb' glances.

Los ripped it open for me. Inside, there were these teeny-weeny jet things which I had to Velcro to my wrists and ankles. The guys were already strapping theirs on and were heavily into an argument about the choice of Phantasy for our Flite.

'How about Icarus – Wings on Fire?' Rio was suggesting. 'That's kinda fun.'

'No, boring,' said Tyrone. 'We did that last week. How about Flight thru Nuclear Holocaust?'

'Justine's never flown before. How about Raiders of the Lost Planet?' said Los. 'Mom's done that one.'

My heart sank. Knowing boys, this was going to be a big opportunity to prove their superiority by terrifying the pants off me. But it was too late now to back out. Los was already checking that I had my jets Velcroed securely.

'Just stick with me and do what I do, OK?' he whispered.

I nodded but I could feel myself coming out in nervous goose-pimples. We were herded along in a queue of kids. The queue ended at a hideous kind of diving-board and beyond that there was *absolutely nothing*. No, seriously, it was this vast void, big enough to house a nest of stacked Millennium Domes. And inside this void, suspended in weightlessness, getting smaller and smaller until they were mere specks in the distance, were *people*.

The others dived off ahead of me, laughing and shouting to each other as they did so. I watched them swooping and gliding as if they'd been born to it. As if *flying* was the most natural thing in the world.

I was left standing there.

Los did a midair back-flip and flew back to me. 'Just jump,' he said. 'It's easy.'

I stood on the end of the board, having what I reckon amounted to an out-of-body experience. On the one hand, there I was, psyching myself up to jump. On the other I was tempted to do what any sane and normal person would in my position – turn tail and head straight back to the locker room.

'What's wrong? You're holding everyone up!' shouted Rio.

I couldn't bring myself to do it. And I wanted so hard not to let Los down in front of his mates. But I was paralysed with fear, glued to the spot. I stood there for what felt like forever, trying to summon the courage. And then a small boy in the queue behind me gave me a shove and whether I had the courage or not, I took off. That's when the 'virtual' kicked in.

I found myself flying through clouds at first and then they cleared and I saw the sea glinting giddyingly miles beneath me.

Los flew up beside me and grinned encouragingly. 'Great, isn't it?'

All the others were doing arty loop the loops and incredible swoops and dives. They kept shouting to each other about how brilliant it was. They clearly thought the whole experience was ace, epic, cryonic.

I felt like one of those girl presenters on 'Blue Peter', trying to keep a brave face and be one of the lads, shouting enthusiastically at the camera while practically throwing up from fright.

As we hurtled along I could feel my hair being plastered back in the most unflattering fashion, my eyes were streaming and yes, sure enough, my nose joined in. Any attempt to wipe my nose, sent the jets wildly off-stream and caused me to somersault in the most hair-raising fashion.

Coming out of an accidental double-back flip, I found myself alone in a cloudbank. Los was nowhere to be seen.

That's when the Raiders attacked. I reckon they'd been lying in wait and singled me out as the weakest in the team. All hell let loose at that point, fireballs were bursting all around me.

I battled on, dodging the fire as best I could, and then Los zoomed back out of the blue with some ammunition.

'Come on. You're not even defending yourself!' he shouted as he lobbed a flame-thrower at me.

'How do I work this thing?' I'd gone all fingers and thumbs.

'Undo the safety catch.'

I did and enveloped him in fire. Oops!

'Justine, you're not meant to fire at your own team,' he said as he reappeared through the flames.

'Oh-my-god!' I gasped.

'What's wrong now?'

But I wasn't looking at him. I was staring at this vast alien which had appeared behind him. It had huge pointed teeth dripping with blood and festooned with strands of a disgusting claggy ooze. It was just about to bite Los's head off when I zapped it. It fell from the sky with a classic baddie 'Aaaaargh!'

'Nice one,' said Los. 'Come on, let's try and catch up with the others.'

Easier said than done. They were so far ahead they were out of sight. For the next half-hour I was so busy defending myself that I didn't take in much of the planet we were meant to be saving. And then I started to get a spooky sense that I'd seen it before. Sure enough, within minutes we were circling the Eiffel Tower. I watched it buckle and subside into a heap of twisted scrap metal as it took a direct hit from an alien missile. The next thing I knew, we were zooming between the columns of the Acropolis and aliens were attacking from all sides. The air was filled with unearthly screams and howls; I just kept zapping randomly and was rewarded by showers of blood and guts pouring from the sky.

Eventually there was nothing left to zap. All I could see were fires burning across a desolate landscape dotted with the odd bit of charred temple. So I gave up on Greece and I flew on.

I caught up with Los over the pyramids. His flame-thrower had received a dead hit and dangled in pieces in his hand. I zapped a couple more aliens as they came in for the kill.

'You're brilliant at this, Justine,' he gasped, scraping alien guts out of his eyes.

'What's happened to the others?'

'They got bored. Decided to skip Asia. They wanted to play something with a bit more action.'

Personally, I didn't blame them. The Velcro was cutting into my wrists, my back ached and every muscle in my body was complaining about this totally unnatural form of exercise. Besides, I wanted to quit while the going was good.

'What happens if we give up now?' I shouted.

'Give up? We haven't saved the US yet.'

'OK. America and then that's it.'

'Catch up with me in New York,' said Los and he zoomed on ahead.

It took ages to defend America, there was so much of it and there seemed to be an endless supply of aliens. This just wasn't fair. The more I zapped, the more appeared.

Making a last ginormous effort, I caught up with Los again. He was sitting getting his breath back on a ledge with his legs dangling, at the very top of the Empire State Building. I homed in and perched myself beside him.

'I reckon we've done a pretty good job,' I said.

He nodded.

Below us the grid of streets was clogged with dead aliens. Police sirens rang out eerily and you could see the tiny ant-like forms of pedestrians emerging out on to the sidewalks. The traffic was starting to weave its way through the gridlock and I could see dump-trucks clearing away the carnage. The planet was getting back to normal.

'What's our score?'

'Not as good as last time I played. But considering it was your first time, you weren't bad for a beginner.'

'Not bad? I saved your life I don't know how many times!'

'Mostly I was fending them off before they got to you.'

'Oh yeah. So how many did you zap?'

'Wasn't keeping count. Any rate, loads more than you . . .'

'You couldn't have . . .'

We were so deep in our argument that neither of us noticed one last stray alien creeping up on us.

With an ear-splitting detonation we were both engulfed in fire.

Sirens screamed all around us and the message Game Over flashed up before my eyes.

I suddenly found I was back, suspended in midair in the Air-o-drome. Los was floating beside me.

'Now look what you've done!' he said.

'Me!'

'Well, I couldn't zap him. He was behind me.'

'Weren't you the one who was so *brilliant* at defending me?'

'I thought you said you could defend yourself.'

'Oh, thanks a lot!'

'It's getting late anyway,' said Los with a grin. 'And it's Saturday night.'

'Saturday night?'

He flew closer and whispered in my ear: 'Saturday nights, that's when the cool crowd goes down the tube to Downside.'

14

By the time we emerged from the Air-o-drome, the simulated sunset was streaking the sky with crimson. I climbed into the verticator, wondering when the weird post-flite sensation would wear off. I still felt as though I was flying – my knees had turned to jelly.

Some guys at the back were muttering about the night ahead. It seemed they had plans that they didn't want other people to hear.

'What's going on?' I whispered to Los.

'There's a load of us going Downside.'

'What are we going to do down there?'

Los looked nervously over his shoulder. 'Look around. Do some site-seeing.'

'Aren't we going to meet up with the . . .' I leaned a little closer, 'you-know-who?'

'Maybe. Dunno.'

'Can't we eat first? I'm starving.'

'Could do. There's a cool restaurant down there. They've got a vintage menu and all.'

'Sounds good.'

'We'll have to switch to another descent mode though.'

Things were looking up. Los was planning a meal out – in a proper restaurant this time. That was positive. And he couldn't call me an airbrain any longer. Not when I had the answers to the entire A-level Advanced Maths syllabus at my fingertips . . . Hey – that's a thought! Chuck's equation. I probably knew the answer already. Now, what was it he'd asked for exactly . . .? Was it the unified theory of the complete universe? Or was it the complete theory of the unified universe? Or the universal theory of . . . I'd have to call him up and ask. I thought 'Chuck' and sure enough the little picture of him appeared in the corner of my visual field.

'Justine!'

'What?'

'Who's the dweeby guy in the crap hat?' asked Los. He was cross-posting with my e-mail.

'Just a friend.'

'Chuck,' he said thoughtfully. 'Wasn't he the one you said you were hanging out with?'

I pulled away from him. 'Frankly, I would prefer, in future, if you didn't snoop on my thoughts, if you don't mind.'

'Up to you. Most people like to stay on-line.'

'I'm not most people.'

'I know. I've noticed. If you don't like it, switch off, then.'

'How?'

'See the on-line icon? Think Off.'

I did, instantly realising that cutting him off from reading my thoughts meant that I couldn't read his. But quite frankly this was a small price to pay for privacy. Chuck would just have to wait for his dweeby equation. We continued our journey in both mental and verbal silence for a while.

Down below in Central 7777, we found the concourse practically deserted.

'So where is everyone?'

Los held a finger to his lips. 'It's a few minutes to curfew.'

The few last stragglers had broken into a run, speeding down the conveyors at breakneck speed. I could hear the curfew siren ringing in my ears.

'What'll happen if we get caught?'

'We won't if we hurry. Follow me.'

It was late evening, the last of the low artificial sunset was sending shafts of light down the malls. Our figures cast long eerie shadows down the walkways. As the sun faded and the gloom gathered, I could hear our footsteps echoing in the emptiness of the place. Just the two of us.

At least, I think it was just the two of us. The echoes were playing tricks with me, I kept on thinking I could hear someone following us.

I paused and listened. 'Did you hear that?'

'Hear what?'

'Footsteps. I thought I heard someone behind us.'

Los swung round and strode back a few steps then returned to me. 'No, you're imagining things. No one there.'

He slipped down a narrow causeway and I followed. I found him waiting for me beside this massive steel tube thing that led downwards through the core of the tower.

We were outside what looked like a service lift. It was built of heavy-duty steel, a kind of cage, bolted with giant-sized greasy bolts. Reminded me a bit of Chelsea Bridge. Positively Victorian.

'Looks a bit old-fashioned,' I whispered.

'Downside technology,' said Los. 'It's not biotech, it's not even on digital. But unlike the stuff up here, it's reliable.' With that he pulled on a heavy steel handle which gave with a resounding 'clunk'.

The concertina doors slid open. He stepped inside. I peered

into the murky depths. The whole space was taken up with stacks of sealed metal containers. It smelled simply frightful.

'What are they?'

'What do they look like? Rubbish.'

'If you think I'm travelling in a garbage shaft, you can think again.'

'Come on. They're all sealed. They can't do you any harm.'

'Why can't we go in a proper "verticator"?'

'This way we can dodge Security. No questions asked. Come on.'

I stepped inside and he slammed the concertina doors behind us. With a squeal of cable on metal, the lift set in motion. It was pitch dark inside.

At the far end, some rubbish shifted and subsided. I jumped.

'What was that?'

'Nothing. Something fell.'

'I don't like this.'

'This is nothing. Wait till you get Downside.'

My heart sank. This was obviously going to be the equivalent of boys taking you on ghastly camping trips up freezing mountains or on disgusting expeditions down oozing potholes to see if you can pass the being-one-of-the-lads test.

'I'm cold,' I complained.

'Come a bit closer, then.' He put an arm round me.

(Typical boy. Absolutely no sense of time and place.)

'Warmer now?'

'A bit.'

He put his other arm round me.

(OK, who cared if we were currently in a vertically-orientated garbage truck? I hadn't had a lot of opportunities like this recently. We were close and it was dark and we were alone together at last.)

Suddenly I was tired of all the games I'd been playing: like trying to make him jealous (which hadn't worked); and trying to impress him (which hadn't either); and playing hard to get (which even I couldn't take seriously). The time had come to face facts. This was important. This was for real. Besides, I might never have a chance like this again.

'Los?' I said.

'Mmmm?' he drew me closer still.

OK, deep breath – basically, it was now or never. (Oh how did one say it in a cool way? I racked my brains for other women's great romantic declarations. Claire Danes in *Romeo and Juliet*? Too poetic. Julia Roberts in *Notting Hill*? Too pathetic. Andie McDowell in *Four Weddings and a Funeral*? Too wet. I came to the conclusion that there simply wasn't a cool way. So I blurted it out anyway.

'Los. I think I'm in love with you.'

This was the point at which he should have been knocked out, speechless, barely able to gasp that ever-since-the-very-first-time-he'd-set-eyes-on-me-he'd-been-waiting-for-this-moment. He hadn't had the courage to say it but he loved me too – passionately.

But things never go like they do in the movies, do they?

'Erm,' he said. (Not a good start.)

I waited with a pounding heart.

'You see, the thing is. Upside. We don't actually *believe* in love any more.'

'What?'

'Not any more.'

'What do you mean. You don't "believe" in it?'

'No. You see, it's been proven. There's no such thing. You had tons of weird superstitions back your time. It's just primitive folklore. Just messes everything up, genetically, I mean. In actual fact – it's been banned,' he finished.

'Don't be ridiculous. You can't ban love!'

'No, listen. They have. I mean, they've proved it doesn't exist. Some researchers worked the whole thing out centuries ago. It's just electrical activity in the brain. No more than that.'

'But it's real! It's more real than anything!'

'Prove it.'

'I can't. You can't prove it. You can only feel it.'

'Look. I'm sorry. I can't. What's it like?'

'What's it like?'

'Yes. Tell me? I'd really like to know.'

(What was it like? God, I'd spent most of my waking life thinking about it, hadn't I? I should be an expert.)

'Well . . . when it's going well . . .' I started.

'Hmmm.'

'. . . And the other person is around. It's like you're on an all-time high. Colours are more vivid. Music sounds brilliant. Your whole body is kind of bathed in . . . I don't know, super-reality . . .'

'That'll be serotonin. Or rather serotonin withdrawal. Serotonin's a chemical. You can simulate it. A few ml. should put you right.'

'No listen. It's not something you can cure that easily. It's true human feelings. When things go badly you feel that life's not worth living. You'd rather be dead.'

'Withdrawal symptoms. Definitely addictive. No wonder they banned it.'

'No! It's not chemical. It's real!'

'Fairy stories, Justine.'

'No! It's the most important thing there is. I can't believe you're saying these things.'

'No need to get so worked up about it.'

Worked up! Of course I was worked up! He was saying he didn't love me. No, worse. He was saying that he could never love me. Because there was no such thing as love.

How many Agony Aunts would it take to change this? Agony Aunts! Bollocks! You can give up on advice, man. Burn the book! No one had an answer to a problem like mine.

15

The lift was slowing. It screeched to a halt. Los leaned over and swung back the clamp on the door. The great concertina doors slid open.

We seemed to be in some sort of hideous refuse depot. All I could make out were shadowy mountains of stacked containers. The air was filled with the stench of rotting garbage.

'What's wrong?' asked Los, catching sight of my face.

'Nothing.'

'You just look a bit down, that's all.'

I decided to blame my current mood on the venue. 'Well, it's not exactly soft lights and sweet music around here, is it?'

There was a rough-looking guy wearing orange coveralls outside. He had a rake and was sifting through the rubbish. He did a double-take when he saw us.

'Hey, where d'you think you're goin'?' he shouted and he lifted his rake threateningly.

'Hold it,' said Los and he held out a hand and grasped the guy's free hand in his, linking fingers with him. 'Onward and Outward,' he said. It was the strange kind of greeting I'd heard him use before – with those guys he hung out with in my time who were in the band with him.

The guy unfroze and grinned. 'Onward and Outward,' he repeated. He nodded his head in my direction. 'She with you?'

'If it's OK.'

'It's OK by me. Don't know what they'll make of her if they pick you up in an ID check.'

'We'll sort that out when the time comes.'

'Good luck, then.'

'What was all that Onward and Outward stuff?' I asked when we were out of earshot.

'Cyberian greeting.'

'Is everyone Downside in the cult?'

'No, not everyone. Just people who want a few things changed down here.'

Changed! I could see why. What a dump! The ground was uneven under my feet. It felt like walking on dead dogs. And it was slippery too. Almost before I knew it I'd stepped straight into a puddle.

'What is this place? Why did you want to come here? It's horrid. Why can't we take a pod?'

'They don't have pods Downside.'

'My feet are wet.'

'Just hang on to me and I'll soon get you to some transport.'

Los was feeling his way up some kind of stairway. As my eyes adjusted I could make out the occasional strip of metal beneath my feet. The stairway was steep and narrow. There was a handrail that crumbled under my hand – felt like perished rubber.

Up at the top, we came out into an open space. We were under some sort of arched roof supporting panes of shattered glass. We'd arrived on a curving slab of cracked and pitted concrete. I could make out other shadowy figures waiting on it. Below, a long swerve of steel rails glinted in the moonlight. It was all somehow weirdly familiar.

That's when I caught sight of an Underground sign. It was so corroded with rust you could barely make out the name: London Bridge.

'Oh my god! We're in London.'

'These days, they call it Londown.'

'Lon*down*?'

' "Londown because it's run–down" as the saying goes.'

'So London's still here?'

'Yes and no.'

Saturday night in London! Let's face it, the centre was bound to be more civilised than this. A night out on the town. And a whole millennium on. I wondered how the nightlife scene had evolved. I stared up the line, waiting for the familiar whine and rumble of a train approaching. Mind you, of course, after a thousand years or so tube trains must've been modernised beyond all recognition. By now they probably had cool little individual TVs like they do in club class air travel.

Sure enough, after a few minutes there was something coming down the line. But it looked too small to be a train. It moved with an odd rhythmic clanking sound.

As it drew nearer I could make out figures leaning back and forth in a rowing motion. Some sort of rickety maintenance vehicle was being winched along the rails, manually.

'Dangerous,' I commented. 'What if there were a train coming?'

'Train?' said Los. 'This is the train.'

The vehicle came to a halt and everyone made a dash for it, fighting to get on.

'Come on. We don't want to get left behind,' said Los.

He held out a hand to help me across the gap. Whatever it

was was balanced precariously on the rails. It rocked violently as people scrambled aboard. Los managed to secure enough room for the two of us towards the back.

A guy in the front of me shoved a long pole into my hand. 'What's this for?' I asked

'What'cha think it's for?' he answered roughly.

He slid his pole out over the side. On the count of five, everyone gave a massive push and the 'train' started, jerkily clanking into motion.

'Do I have to?' I whispered to Los.

'Anything to help speed it up,' he said.

'What's happened to the proper tube trains?' (Run-down was putting it mildly.)

'There aren't any "proper" trains any longer. You haven't seen anything yet.'

I peered forwards into the darkness with misgivings. The tube without a tube train was pitch black and eerie. Water dripped from the ceiling and I wondered if something worse was about to fall on me.

As we penetrated deeper into the maze of tunnels, one of the guys up front lit a kind of flare so we could dimly make out where we were going.

The journey was agonisingly slow, with umpteen stops for no apparent reason. We spent ages sitting staring at a load of sooty snaking cables for what felt like for ever. In fact, it was very much like any Saturday night back my time. I could swear, only a week ago, I'd been seated for a good quarter of an hour facing the very same box that had 'LT outlet. Staff only' stencilled across it. But at last we got going again. As we made our painful progress forward I could dimly make out that we were passing stations. But these were deserted and cloaked in darkness and our 'train' showed no sign of stopping to let people off.

At last, we arrived at one station which seemed to be in operation. By the flickering light of the front guy's flare I could make out the shadowy faces of people waiting on a platform. And behind them, under the centuries of graffiti which encrusted the walls like some futuristic sort of lichen, there was a tube sign which read *PIC AD LY CIRC S*.

'Right,' said Los. 'Get ready to jump. This is where we get off.'

At least it was somewhere I knew. I thought nostalgically of the Criterion Brasserie. I'd been there for a really yummy slap-up meal with Franz and her dad. But they were bound to have had umpteen changes of chef by now and the place, no doubt, would have gone right downhill.

Once the train had gone, the total pitch blackness of the station was only relieved by the occasional person lighting a match. I clung to Los for dear life. The crowd was silent, concentrated, moving upwards with shuffling steps. We felt our way up blindly like moles searching for a way out.

It was a relief at last to feel fresh air on my face. As we neared the surface, through the general gloom and grime I made out the entrance to the Virgin Megastore. I'd been wondering how the music scene had moved on . . .

But it was dark inside. Not open, by the look of it. And instead of racks of glossy, pristine CDs, I could make out the dim shapes of tents and bedrolls and shadowy people moving about in the gloom. Up one more flight of steps and we found ourselves in what should have been Piccadilly Circus.

I looked up to where the big jolly Lucozade bottle eternally emptied and refilled itself. There were just a few stark ribs of torn metal outlined against the sky. There wasn't a Sony logo either, or that little yellow strip of news headline that went round and round for ever as if by magic.

'What's happened to all the lights?'

'There haven't been lights here for centuries,' said Los.

But there was light – firelight. And it lit up a grim landscape of makeshift shelters. Feral-looking people were outlined against the raw flames of bonfires. The air smelled of acrid smoke and burning food. As my eyes became accustomed to the darkness, I became aware of what kind of people they were. They were Fourth Millennium equivalents of what looked like eco-warriors. It was all beards, beanies and balaclavas, and wild-haired girls in retro gear, very long and randomly ripped.

Already a group of youngish ones had gathered around Los. Most of these were dressed like him in black stuff. They Hi-fived him with fingers linked in that same greeting he'd given the worker at the depot. 'Onward and Outward.'

Several of them eyed me up and down but made no comment. But I was staring at them. Physically, they weren't at all like the people Upside. Underneath their ragged clothing they were the kind of crowd you'd see hanging out anywhere on a Saturday night, my time. It was a bit of a relief to see all their random varieties of body shape as a matter of fact. There was even the standard guy with the spots and dweeby hairstyle that you get on every night out. And there was a rather pretty girl, of the low-kneed, duck-arsed variety, who had a guy with his arm round her. No one – absolutely no one – was perfect. Apart from Los, that is.

But I wasn't the only one to have noticed. Just about all of the girls kept eyeing him. I moved a possessive step closer. Down here, at any rate, he was my property.

'So where's this cool vintage restaurant of yours?' I asked.

'Not far,' said Los.

He led me down what must once have been Regent Street. I could just make out the dim shapes of fallen columns sticking out from the rubble. One of them was being used horizontally to prop up the roof of some kind of makeshift shelter.

In front of this was a wooden sign with rough characters scratched on to it:

> *Heritage site*
> *Please treat with respect*
> *And use the rubbish receptors prov'd.*

16

Beneath the tarnished arches, just visible in the gloom, stood an aged grimy figure. His plastic was time-soiled and showed fatigue cracks – and he'd lost his jolly red nose somewhere along the way. But you could still tell it was Ronald McDonald all right.

'Inspiring, isn't it?' said Los with a quick intake of breath. His voice had the kind of hollow awed quality people back my time reserved for a trip round a place like Hampton Court or Westminster Abbey. And, come to think of it, there was a bit of half-timbering supporting the roof.

'I like the cool Tudor effect,' I said.

'It's all authentic, same millennium,' said Los, going up to a beam and stroking the woodwork. 'Look, it's real wood – it's even got genuine . . . What do'ya call these tiny holes?'

'Woodworm?'

'Mmmm. 'Mazing.'

'Come on, it's only wood.'

Los dragged himself away and we joined the queue that led into the gloomy depths of the place. Standing patiently in the flickering candlelight, the people ahead of us were silent and respectful. There was none of the standard McDonald's jostling and queue-barging. They stood aside to let the people who'd already been served pass by with reverence. What with the candles and everything, it all felt a bit like being in church.

Some Upsiders who were in the queue ahead of us were peering at a menu which was chalked up on the wall.

'Not even say how many kcals,' one girl complained.

'What is beef?' asked another.

'Dunno, I suss it's some animal derivative,' said the boy with them.

The girls expressed horror. 'Not you mean they consume animals down here? Non positive!'

I think Los was somewhat overawed when it came to the point of ordering. The menu was basic McDonald's fare but it was quite beyond him. He got in a right old muddle between the sizes of fries and didn't know the difference between a Big Mac and a Quarter Pounder, so I took over and sorted the whole thing out and told the girl serving that neither of us wanted gherkin.

'What's gherkin?' Los whispered as we took our tray and slid on to two facing bench seats.

'It's a nasty slimy little green bit. You wouldn't like it.'

'How do you know?'

'Trust me. I know.'

He bit into his burger and chewed thoughtfully. 'I bet everybody else's got gherkin,' he said.

'Will you stop going on about it?'

'Well, still . . .' he shrugged.

His eye lit on a couple over the way. The girl had taken the gherkin out of her burger and was feeding it to the guy opposite. You know the way girls do when they want to make up to a bloke? Ritual feeding and all that.

Los bit into his burger with a sigh. He'd gone really sulky.

'OK, OK. I'll get you some gherkin, if it means so much to

you. Wait here,' I said.

Luckily the queue wasn't so long this time.

'Could I have two slices of gherkin, please?' I asked the girl.

She looked really taken aback. 'Just gherkin?'

'Well, yes.'

'We'll have to make a charge.'

'For gherkin?'

'It's earth-grown organic gherkin.'

'But we didn't have it in our Big Macs. Couldn't we just have the two slices we didn't have?'

The logic of this was totally beyond her. 'No, you have to pay. Your order's already been processed.'

'All right then, I'll pay.' Even earth-grown organic gherkin couldn't cost a fortune, could it? But hang on, what was I going to do for money?

'It's OK. I'll deal with it.' Los had come up behind me. He handed over a chip. The girl held it up to a candle to check if it was genuine, then nodded. She carefully spread out two wafer-thin slices of gherkin in a McDonald's box.

'You want one?' asked Los.

'No. I don't like gherkin.'

Los slipped a slice into his mouth and closed his eyes. 'Mmmm.'

'You like it?'

'Brilliant. Made it worth coming here. There's nothing like real earth-grown food.'

I got up from the table to take our empty containers to the bins. I reached for Los's burger box and drinks carton.

'Wait,' he said. He extricated the little plastic paddle that serves as a spoon and put it into his top pocket. 'Souvenir,' he whispered and patted the pocket.

There were buskers playing outside McDonald's, a guy and a

girl. They had a beanie on the ground and Upsiders were throwing the odd chip in as they passed by.

Los immediately headed over to them.

There was a load of 'Long-time-no-see' and 'Wha-you-bin-man?' and back slapping from the guy. I hovered in the shadows, waiting for an opportunity to break into the circle and make my presence felt.

I was distracted by a sudden harsh 'Pssst!'

It was the dodgy dealer we'd seen Upside. 'You wanna buy cigarettes?' he hissed in that standard gangster manner, lips clenched, head averted.

'No,' I said. Any moment now, Los would turn and catch us. I wasn't going to let something as insubstantial as a cigarette come between us. 'Go away.'

But he wasn't going to be put off so lightly. 'I make you good deal. Wanted them back there, lady. You wanted them badly.'

'So? Just maybe I've given up since,' I said with determination. 'Will you please leave me alone.'

Los had finished talking to the others and was beckoning to me. With a glance in his direction, the guy disappeared in the crowd. Los hadn't seen him. He was too wrapped up in his friends.

'Hey, Justine, come over. Look who it is.'

'We met before,' said the guy. 'Remember me? Phil? We met back your time.'

I hadn't recognised them in the gloom. They were the two who'd been in the band with Los.

They were wearing T-shirts with the band's name on: LOVE – Lords Of Virtual Existence.

I tugged at Los's sleeve. 'Aren't these people with the Cyberians?' I whispered.

He nodded and signalled that I should keep it to myself.

'And TeXas,' he said, pulling the girl forward.

'Justine,' she said, with that Mona Lisa smile of hers. 'What are you doing here?'

'Just came for the weekend.'

'Time-tourist, eh? Come to see the sites?'

I ignored the barb in her voice and said, 'I can't believe how much everything's changed.'

She nodded grimly. 'Picturesque, isn't it?'

Phil turned to Los. 'Look, we've got a gig on tonight. Why don't you join us? We thought we might play some, er . . .' He cast a nervous glance over his shoulder. *'Love* ballads.'

'Where?'

'This evil place I know, back out west.'

'What you doing for power?' asked Los.

'We've fixed that,' said Phil with a grin. 'At least, we've got adequate.'

'Cryonic. Let's get over there.'

'What about her?' asked TeXas, giving me a look that could kill.

'We can't just leave her here,' said Phil.

'She can come along,' said Los. 'Why not?'

'Four people in a three man band?'

'OK, so let's give her something to do.'

All this time I had been listening to the conversation with some concentration. A gig. Now, I've always fancied myself as a bit of a singer. There was a time when Franz, Henry, Max and I were seriously planning on forming our own girl band. We'd got as far as nearly ringing up EMI and offering to make a demo. We saw ourselves as a kind of up-market version of the Spice Girls. Not that any of us could sing or anything. But we had attitude and that was the crucial part.

Now all eyes fell on me. I cleared my throat, realising that this could well be the opportunity I'd been waiting for. I was about to make my big break.

'So, do you play?' asked Phil.

'Oh yes, sure.'

'What do you play?' asked TeXas.

'Errm, guitar mostly.' (Chuck had painstakingly taught me a few chords one wet Bank Holiday Monday.)

'We've got my spare acoustic,' said Phil.

'That'll do,' said Los. 'How far is it?'

''Bout three k.'

'And the traffic's bound to be ghastly on a Saturday night,' I said.

Phil let out a dry sort of laugh. 'Doesn't she know anything?'

I glanced down Piccadilly. This time on a Saturday night the traffic should've been at a standstill in a good old traditional jam. But there wasn't a single bit of viable transport in sight.

'Where are all the taxis?' I asked.

'Taxis?' TeXas stared at me as if I was the dumbest thing on two legs.

'You know, shiny black things with little yellow lights on top?' I said as cuttingly as I could manage.

'Fossil fuels ran out centuries ago,' said Los.

'What have fossils got to do with it?'

Phil sighed. 'No oil? No petrol? No traffic.'

'Oh, we're not going to have to go on that train thing again, are we?'

'Uh uh,' said Phil. 'We'll take the limo. It's waiting outside the Ritz.

The Ritz had definitely gone downhill. Most of the windows were boarded over and there was a line of grimy washing strung across Piccadilly. And outside, instead of that nice uniformed porter who opened car doors for all the VIPs, there was a guy in uniform who asked to see our passes.

'We've got immunity, mate. We're musicians,' said Phil.

'What about her?' he said, indicating me. 'A droid musician? That'll be a first.'

'Droid technology's come on a long way,' said Los.

The guy looked at me and smirked. 'Yeah, I wouldn't mind playing with her either.'

I gave him a look that could kill and stayed close to Los.

The others were already climbing aboard a strange contraption that looked like a particularly nasty pile-up from the Tour de France. It consisted of umpteen wheels and pedals and had a kind of trailer in tow behind it.

'Pedalimo,' said Phil, stroking its handlebars with the kind of affection guys had for classic cars back my time. 'With decent outriders it can reach up to thirty k.p.h.'

I climbed up beside Los, hoping that cycling together, though obviously wet and uncomfortable, would at least prove bonding. As soon as we were all aboard we were surrounded by a load of boys who wanted to come along for the ride. Phil selected six of the biggest and strongest lads and they took up the outrider positions. After a bit of argument with the ones who'd been rejected for the trip, the vehicle took off.

We sped along beneath the vast plane trees which bordered Green Park. There was a scent of woodsmoke in the air and I could just make out the ramshackle shapes of a kind of shantytown of straw-bale huts lurking between the trees, looking incredibly organic and mud-clogged and ever-so-smugly self-sufficient. As we skirted Hyde Park Corner a small herd of goats ran alongside us. It was the kind of London all those Green people back my time would wet their cycle capes over – all scrupulously lead-free, with sound and light pollution down to an all-time low. What they simply didn't realise was that 'the good life' is so incredibly slow, exhaustingly hard work and so awfully smelly.

Once we were beyond the nice downhill bit that led into Knightsbridge, the going got harder. You simply don't notice that London has slopes from inside a car. And these slopes were rutted and lumpy, with potholes in them that we had to keep skirting round. So we cycled twice as far as we should have done. My muscles were already sore from flying. Now faced with yet another taxing form of exercise they were crying out for mercy. Basically I was becoming all too aware of the fact that I hadn't slept the night before.

TeXas was peddling stolidly with an intent look on her face. She caught me freewheeling and gave me a look that could kill. I glared back and made a big act of standing up on the pedals and pushing for all I was worth.

'What's up with you and TeXas?' whispered Los.

'We don't exactly hit it off.'

'I noticed. Why?'

'She's so arrogant for a Downsider.'

'Oh, she's not really a Downsider.'

'She's not?'

'She's an Upsider who's dropped out. Joined the Cyberians, and came down here to be with Phil. Her moms are going crazy. They can't understand it.'

Nor could I, frankly. Imagine wanting to live on a rubbish tip when you could be living Upside, where it was clean and dry and civilised and where everything didn't smell of manure. Of course, we had girls like her back my – time – who went off inexplicably in vans overland to ever-so-ethnic places and who only communicated ever after with their families by postcard.

The going got easier at that point and we all had a welcome break freewheeling. I realised that we must be in Knightsbridge.

But where was Knightsbridge? The acres of glossy shopfronts had totally disappeared. All that was left were humungous piles of rubble through which our rutted track wove its dismal way. My eye was automatically drawn to one of the mounds in particular and I came to the bitter realisation that this must be all that was left of Harvey Nix.

It was a really weird feeling, actually, to be pedalling down a street which wasn't there any more. We were currently going in the direction of Harrod's, which wasn't there either. And beyond that should be Chelsea and my home which, without doubt, had totally gone as well.

Normally, on a Saturday night, home was the very last place I'd want to be. But the thought of it not being there brought on a massive attack of nostalgia. I thought of Fred Bear, abandoned and cold and mouldering in the rubble. Then I comforted myself with the thought that he'd probably been auctioned umpteen times by now and would no doubt be preserved in some museum for incredibly rare and valuable antique bears.

I turned to Los. 'Where are we going? Where is there to go?'

'What do you mean?'

'There's nothing left. No bars, no cafés, no clubs. Nothing.'

'Sure there is,' he said. 'Cheer up. Phil's taking us to this evil place. You'll love it. It's all original Second Millennium.'

17

The 'evil' place Phil knew turned out to be a pub. One of those fake olde worlde gin palaces, all false beams, latticed windows and horse brasses, like you find in incredibly dull suburbs. But come 3001, it seemed it had become the ultimate in cool.

The saloon bar was packed with alternative-looking types standing shoulder to shoulder in the half-light. There was a lot of commando gear, rolled woolly caps and beards of every conceivable length, type and colour. They were smoking stuff that reeked of bonfires and they were drinking what looked like beer out of pint mugs. But you could see from the steam that was rising from the glasses that whatever was inside was hot.

Phil leaned over the bar. 'What've you got?' he asked the barmaid with a raised eyebrow.

'Juice,' she said, giving him a very straight look.

'Orange?'

'Yeah.' She glanced towards the door and added in an undertone, 'Pekoe.'

'That'll do,' said Phil.

She filled four pint mugs from a steaming urn and slid them

across to him. Phil picked his up and started to shoulder his way across the room to where a rickety stage had been set up at the far end.

'What is it?' I whispered to Los.

He cast a glance around the room. 'Tea,' he hissed back.

'Oh wicked!' I'd been dying for a cuppa ever since I'd arrived. I turned to the barmaid. 'You don't have milk and sugar by any chance, do you?'

'What are you?' she sneered. 'Some lightweight?'

A bartender came out from a back room, wiping his hands on an oily rag. 'You made it,' he said to Phil.

Phil nodded. 'What's happened to the power? Thought you were fixing that.'

'They're taking a break. I'll give 'em a shout,' said the guy.

He went out the back and started bawling at someone. His call was answered with a chorus of groans. But within seconds, glimmering dully at first and dying out and then lighting up again and gaining strength, the lighting system struggled into life.

There was a muted roar of approval as people shaded their eyes, blinking in the unaccustomed glare.

'Don't get too used to it. We're looking for volunteers for the treadmill for the late shift,' growled the bartender and he slopped down the bar with his greasy rag.

I sank a little further into the crowd. Personally, I'd had enough exertion for one day.

Los was busy up on the stage, plugging in the keyboard. He tried a couple of notes. They slurred agonisingly.

'Needs more power,' said Phil, and the guy gave another shout out back. There were more groans but the lights brightened.

'Where's that guitar? Hey, Justine. Can you just come in when I give you the nod?' Los asked me.

151

'What do you want me to play?'

'Just improvise.'

I swallowed. 'Sure. No problem,' I said, taking the guitar, just praying I was holding it the right way round.

With a great clashing chord Los broke into an intro and Phil started up on the drums. TeXas kind of wailed.

The audience went mad, stomping their feet and whistling.

Was this music? Or were they just tuning up? I mean, I guess music must've moved on a bit. I mean moved on a lot. But not this far. It wasn't a bit like they'd played my time. Even if I could have remembered the chords, there was no way I could play to this.

There was a pause and all eyes rested on me.

'What are you waiting for?' hissed TeXas.

I swallowed.

Los gave me the nod again.

I took a deep breath. I played my three chords. The first was kind of OK. Not absolutely sure if I was quite on the beat but . . . I managed the second as well, but the third went terribly wrong with a painful jarring sound. Amplified against the sudden breathless silence it sounded excruciating.

For a second I waited for abuse or bottles or worse to be hurled. Then Phil said, 'Yeah!' and the others crashed in. Suddenly the audience was going totally crazy.

Los nodded to me to come in again.

I bit my lip and concentrated hard and managed somehow to replicate the same jarring sound.

TeXas took up my tune and wailed soulfully. She started putting words to it. She was singing a love ballad and, like all love ballads, it was a sad one. About how love had gone and how the world didn't-have-no-meaning-no-more. The audience listened in respectful silence. The ballad came to a close with an ear-splitting solo from Phil on drums.

As the last note faded every single person was up on his or her feet. They were stamping on the floor, whistling and whooping, yelling for more.

We played the piece through again, and again. The audience was with us now. Arms were waving in a sea of movement, they simply wouldn't let us go.

It all came to an end with a dimming of the lights. It seemed that the blokes out the back had had enough.

Los turned to the audience and said into the mike, 'That's all, folks.'

'Well done,' he said to me. 'You were brilliant!'

I can't say I deserved credit for my performance. But I accepted the praise with due modesty.

People were already making a beeline for us, demanding autographs. It seemed that Downside, the band had assumed the status of gods.

'Let's get out of here before we get mobbed,' said Phil.

I couldn't help feeling a slight frisson of thwarted celebrity. Frankly, I wouldn't have minded signing a few autographs and having my picture taken looking terribly exposed and reluctant with Los's arm protectively round me.

But Phil had a point. Two girls in particular were pulling at Los's clothing, trying to tear bits off as souvenirs. Knowing males, this was going to undo all the groundwork I'd done so far.

I started to urge him towards the doors. But it was too late. Girls seemed to be coming out of the woodwork, up through the floor, they were all over him. There was no shifting him now.

I slumped down on a stool at the bar and sipped my cold black tea. He seemed to have totally forgotten I existed.

'Pssst . . .' someone hissed by my elbow.

I swung round.

'You want cigarettes?' It was the dodgy dealer in the shades again.

I glanced over at Los. The girls were closing in. Get any closer and that redhead would be sitting on his lap!

'Yeah why not?' I said. I could look poised and chilled like the rest of the world, no sweat. I'd feel more in control with a cigarette in my hand.

The guy held up a hand as if to high-five and when our palms met I felt something press into mine. It was a screw of paper formed into a neat cone with something inside.

'Errm . . . How do I pay for this?' I whispered.

'Chips,' he hissed out of the corner of his mouth.

'What?' (Chips is a particularly difficult word to hiss.)

'Chips,' he tried again.

'I don't have any on me right now.'

'I'll remember your face. You owe me one. OK?'

'OK.'

With that he slid away through the crowd.

With a glance in Los's direction, which established that the redhead now actually *was* on his lap – the shameless hussy, I unscrewed the cone. Inside I found one Rizla paper and a few dozen strands of tobacco. I'd never actually rolled a cigarette before. My end result was a lot fatter and looser than I ideally would have planned but it was vaguely cylindrical.

I leaned over and lit it from a near-by candle. The cigarette glowed briefly and died out. So I tried again and took a big puff this time. With the force of an incendiary device the cigarette flamed into life, catching my hair as it did so.

I'd caught Los's attention all right. He dropped the redhead and with three strides he was across the room. He smothered the fire and stamped out the cigarette.

'What the hell did you think you were doing?' he hissed.

He was positively shaking with anger. Talk about overreacting.

'It was only a cigarette. Other people in here are smoking.'

'What they're smoking doesn't kill people,' he said. 'Come on, we'd better get out of here before the place gets raided.'

But it was too late. The doors of the bar were already being forced open.

'Vice Squad,' said a voice.

And someone shouted, 'Let's get outta here!'

All hell broke loose at that point. Half the people were trying to build a blockade and the rest were fighting each other to get out through the back room. Then someone doused the candles so the place was thrown into pitch darkness. There was a deafening crash of broken glass as tables were tipped over. I was groping around helplessly in the crush when I felt strong arms around me and I found Los was dragging me across the room. We escaped into a dank stairway and stood getting our breath back.

'Look, there's a window halfway up, let's try that,' whispered Los.

The window was jagged with broken glass but we forced it open. Los went first and I heard him drop down the other side.

'Come on, I'll catch you,' he hissed up.

I followed and sure enough he caught me. He set off at a run. I panted after him.

'Where are we going?'

'Back Upside. That's if we can make it before they've alerted Security.'

18

It was a clear night and the moonlight was bright enough to light our way. But also bright enough to be seen by. So we kept to the shadows, dodging from one bit of cover to another. Los seemed to know his way. I followed him through the desolate streets. He slipped through alleyways, finding invisible pathways through rows of tumbledown buildings. Where once there had been neat suburban gardens there were now dense thickets of woodland and weed-strewn mountains of rubble that we had to battle our way through.

Eventually, my heart pounding in my chest, he led me out into the open. He was stumbling on ahead across the desolate remains of a collapsed overhead freeway.

'I can't go much further,' I gasped.

He turned back and grasped me by the hand, pulling me strongly along with him. 'Look,' he said pointing ahead.

I looked, and saw the endless gleaming facets of the Tower soaring upwards. It stood there, improbably beautiful, impossibly perfect, in stark contrast to the lost desolate landscape all around us.

'How do we go up?' I whispered.

'We can't take a verticator. They'll be watched.'

'All this fuss about one little cigarette?' I said.

Los shook his head. 'It's a bit more than that,' he said. 'I reckon the cigarette was just an excuse for the raid.'

'I don't understand.'

'That guy in the shades, he set you up. I reckon he's been tailing us all along. There's been a crackdown. It's the Cyberians they're after. They want to do away with them once and for all.'

There was a rustle behind us. Los spun round.

A feral cat slunk through the shadows, its eyes reflecting eerily in the darkness.

'We can't talk here,' hissed Los and then he spotted something. 'Look, there's a maintenance cradle. It's worth a try.'

Cradle. The word has a nice safe nursery ring to it. Few words have been so misused. This cradle swayed in the breeze on two insubstantial-looking cables which seemed to go upwards endlessly.

'We can't go up in that!' I said.

'Not all the way,' said Los. 'But we can take it up a couple of k and then we should be able to slip in through a service chute.'

A few minutes later we were in the 'cradle', gliding skywards.

I gritted my teeth and risked a glance over the side. At an incredible speed, I saw the moonlit city slipping away beneath us. Poor old London – no, not London – Londown. The familiar pattern of streets was still discernible, etched like a tiny network of wrinkles on an incredibly old and time-worn face. But that was about all. And now even that was growing fainter and fainter until it faded into nothingness . . .

'Don't look down. Look up,' said Los.

I followed his gaze. Above us, the tower stretched on and

on until it was lost from sight, merging into the clear moonlit sky. All around us it was infinitely dotted with stars.

'Venus,' he said.

'Where?'

'Right here beside me.'

It was his pet name for me. He hadn't called me that since I'd arrived. I felt my heart do a kind of lurch and switch up into a faster gear. I reckon all the chase and stuff had had a bonding effect. Maybe I should give it one last try.

'Los,' I started. 'I'm really going to miss you, you know.'

'Me too,' he said.

'What will happen if they catch us?'

'Oh, I don't know. They'll try and prove that we were with the Cyberians.'

'I still don't understand what the big deal is. The Cyberians are about the tamest cult I've ever come across.'

'Not to Upsiders. There's been this big clampdown. It's all the love stuff they believe in. You know it's been banned. The Cyberians are trying to break down the barriers. They'll even tolerate Upsiders and Downsiders getting together . . .'

'What's wrong with that?'

'It's forbidden. Anyway, it's totally irresponsible. I mean, what if they have kids? They'd be sub-opt . . .' He caught himself midway through the word.

'Sub-optimal.' I finished the word for him.

He nodded. 'So you see, once an Upsider drops out, shacks up with a Downsider like TeXas has for instance, they have to stay down there. They'll never be allowed back Upside.'

'But it's the same for me . . .' I said, as the full truth dawned on me. 'I'd never be allowed to live in your world either, would I?'

Los looked awkward and didn't answer.

'Come on, say it. Admit it. I'm not perfect enough . . .'

'Look, Justine. I like you just the way you are. I've never met a girl like you before . . .'

'Sure,' I said turning away. I was angry now. Angry in that futile way that rages against something you can never change. 'It's just a pity I don't pass the standards test on your precious human conveyor belt. Oh I hate you all. I wish I'd never come.'

'Don't be like that. I'm glad you came.'

'So that you could tell me to my face that we've no future together . . .'

'I didn't say that.'

'Yes you did. Not in so many words. But it's true, isn't it? We could never be together Upside. Not ever.'

I stared up at the night sky. The stars had dimmed and the moon had taken on the kind of murky tone of gone-off cottage cheese. The whole universe had simply stopped having any meaning whatsoever. He'd spelled it out now. I remembered that line from the song he'd written for me:

A billion billion stars shine in my heart
While a billion billion hours keep us apart.

I should have realised from the start. This wasn't just like two people from different countries or cultures, we were more like people from different species or different planets. There was no way we could ever end up together.

Los had that tortured look of his on again. 'Look, Justine. Listen to me. Why do you think I'm with the Cyberians?'

'What have they got to do with it?'

'They want to change things . . . You know they do.'

'But that will take for ever. And I'm only here till six o'clock.'

Los smiled and leaned forwards. 'It's just the wrong time and the wrong place for us, that's all.'

I stared at him. Was this just another of those male 'scared of commitment' excuses? Or did he really care about me after all?

I swallowed and tried to put on a brave face. 'I've got to leave in a few hours. Let's try and enjoy what time we have left.'

We sat in miserable silence for the rest of the journey up.

I was desperately trying to put things in perspective. I tried to imagine what Franz would say: 'Look, Justine. There are plenty more guys out there. Game on.' (She was right.)

I thought of what Henry would say: 'Try to be objective, Justine. You knew the two of you weren't a perfect match.' (So true.)

And of what Max would say: 'Poor babe. You'll get over it. You'll see.' (Sniff.)

And of what Mummy would say: 'I could tell that young man was totally unsuitable from the start.' (Ugghhh!)

Eventually we docked at a heavy steel door marked Refuse Crew Only. It swung back automatically to let the cradle in.

We emerged through a service chute into the central concourse. The place was just catching the first light of a murky simulated dawn. It was artificial sunrise and the end of curfew. But there was no one about. I guessed the Upsiders were all too wasted from their virtual partying to be up yet.

Los held up a warning finger and hesitated for a moment, listening. The only sound was the swish swish swish of the autocleaners polishing the concourse and the sucking sound of the windowipers working their way up and down the transpawalls like pond-creepers on their big suction pads.

'OK. Let's make a move.'

No sooner had I put a foot on a conveyor than a voice rang out: 'Stop right there!'

Two RPs emerged from the gloom. Los grasped my arm. 'Don't say a word. I'll do the talking.'

'ID check,' one said roughly to Los and stared hard into his eyes. 'Empty your pockets.'

As Los did so the little paddle from McDonald's fell out and skittered across the floor. The RP retrieved it with a grim expression. 'So, been on a little trip Downside, eh? Don't try to deny it.'

Los shrugged. 'So? It's not illegal.'

'What you been doing down there?'

'Nothing. Bit of music. Seeing friends.'

'What kind of friends?'

'Just friends.'

'Ever heard of some jerks who call themselves "Cyberians"?'

It was just an eye-flick but they caught the look I cast at Los.

'What if I have?'

'They're trouble. Singing seditious songs. I've heard they've even got a band called LOVE.' He almost spat the word out. 'Disgusting.'

'So?. . . They're Downsiders. They can sing about whatever they like down there. It shouldn't affect us,' said Los.

'As long as they keep themselves to themselves,' said the RP.

The other RP leered in my direction. 'What about her?'

'Can't you see? She's a droid,' said Los.

'OK, on your way.'

But another figure emerged from the shadows. 'A droid who smokes cigarettes?' he said with a smirk.

It was the dodgy Downsider, the one I'd bought the cigarette from.

He took off his shades and looked me in the eyes. I saw

with a shock his blue eyes, his perfect features. This was no Downsider. Los had been right. He must've been planted to tail us.

'I said I'd remember your face,' he said. 'Check her over.'

The first RP produced a gauge like they'd used in the terminal and ran it up and down my body. 'You're right. She's human all right and sub-optimal. Hey, look, he's even had her wired to make her look authentic. Nice try.'

'You know the penalty for bringing a Downsider up here?' said the guy in the shades, shoving Los roughly by the shoulder.

'No look. OK, she's not a droid. I can explain, she's a time-tourist.'

'Make up your mind,' he said.

'No, she is. Look at her, ask her . . .'

'Yes I am. I come from 1998,' I said.

'1998,' the RP sneered. 'Check your facts next time, lady. That far back they didn't even have the technology.'

They were pulling me away from Los.

'But they must have had or I wouldn't be here,' I protested.

'She's a Downsider. No two ways about it.'

'OK, de-wire her. Then take her back down.'

'No listen, you can't,' said Los. 'I've got to get her back to the terminal by six. She's got a time-slot booked. She can't miss that.'

The RPs just laughed at him. 'Thought you're going to give us the slip, eh?' said the guy who had stopped us.

Another RP appeared, carrying a kind of de-studding device like they use in shops to get the security tags out of clothes. He had my ear-studs out in minutes. It didn't hurt physically. It was the knowledge that this was cutting me off from Los that brought tears to my eyes.

'Look, just let us say goodbye,' I begged. 'It's not much to ask.'

The first RP's face softened. 'OK, sixty seconds. Make it quick.'

Los put an arm round me and drew me close.

'What's going to happen?' I whispered.

'They're sending you back Downside.' He thrust a fistful of chips into my hand. 'Take these, you'll need them. I'll get down somehow and come and find you.'

'When? How? What if I miss my time-slot back?'

'I don't know. I'll think of something.'

'But I'll be stranded . . .'

The RPs were getting impatient. We were pulled roughly apart. 'That's enough, come on. Take her down.'

Two RPs took me by the arms and forced me into a verticator with them. I caught one last poignant glimpse of Los as they dragged me inside. He raised his hand in a half gesture.

'Onward and Outward,' he mouthed.

I couldn't be sure but I thought I caught a glimpse of tears in his eyes.

Then the doors slid closed with a swift final zapping noise.

19

'Where are we going?' I asked.

'Down.' It was the kinder RP of the two. His face softened. 'Look, love. Personally, I don't blame you for trying it on.'

'But I'm not trying it on. I am a time-traveller. Why won't anyone believe me? You can't make me go down there. I've come from 1998. You can e-mail people and ask. There must be some way to prove it. Like, I don't know who – the police or the passport office or something?'

He just laughed and said to the other RP, 'Listen to it. They'll try anything. I'd just keep quiet if I was you. You'll only make it worse for yourself.'

When the verticator slid to a stop, I was led out into a steel corridor with grim cells leading off it. The air smelled of sickly disinfectant and rang with the hollow sounds of meal cans clanking, shouts of inmates, and other ominously authentic prison noises.

'Where are we?'

'RPHQ,' he said.

He led me over to a vacant cell. It was lined with greasy matt steel and had a low metal bench along one side. One corner was curtained off by a tattered plastic curtain.

'In there,' he said. 'Shouldn't take long.'

A female RP was in the room, she stood against the wall, feet apart in the traditional female jailor manner. A second came in with a wand thing in her hand.

'I've been sent to de-clothe you,' she said.

The one who was standing by the wall gave her a nod and she took me behind the curtain. I felt a low, subsonic buzzing run down my back as she slit the suit open. With a kind of ooze of relief my body slid back into its original shape. I was left to get dressed in some hideous drab kind of prison clothes. I wanted to keep my mules but the RP took them from me.

'You won't be needing these no more,' she said.

'What are they going to do to me?' I asked miserably.

'Nothing. Just take you down, back where you came from.'

'But I'm not a Downsider.'

'Oh don't start that again.'

It seemed their minds were closed on the subject, so I asked, 'What about the guy I was with? What will they do to him?'

'The one who tried to get you up there? Simple. He'll be monitored round the clock so they can keep track of his where-abouts. I can tell you. You won't be seeing him for a while.'

We travelled down officially this time, in a grim steel verticator. I stood between the two blank-faced RPs racking my brain for escape tactics. They always make it seem so easy in the movies don't they? Like you've always got some magical string up your sleeve to garrotte people with or there's some random weapon you can rip off the wall to defend yourself with. But the walls of the verticator were totally uniform flat matt steel. Short of banging the two RPs' heads together, I couldn't think of any way out of this one. And they were a lot taller than me.

The verticator came to a halt. The doors slid open. I was thrust out.

I turned to make one last attempt at pleading with them but without a smile or a word they stepped back inside and the doors slid closed with a final-sounding 'thunk'.

I looked around. I didn't even know where I was. All I could make out as far as the eye could see was rubble, rubbish and scrub. A thousand years of obsolete hardware was piled in dun grey mountains, shards of plastics of every colour of the spectrum glittered in the early morning sunlight. There must have been hundreds and hundreds of years of accumulated rubbish under my feet. I'm telling you, it gave a whole new meaning to crushing soft drinks cans and taking bottles to the bottle bank. From now on I was definitely going to write on both sides of every Post-It slip.

I looked back and took one last regretful glance at the Tower. It stood like some great and beautiful beast, casting its long cold shadow over the landscape.

I'd been thrown out. Exiled from everything that was perfect and glossy and new and beautiful. I couldn't be with Los because I wasn't glossy and new and beautiful enough. I was just an obsolete human from an outmoded millennium and I'd been trashed. I'd never felt so desolate before. My eyes filled with tears. Basically, I was going to have to give up trying to have a happy life.

I didn't even want to live Upside. What was the point if they'd abolished the only thing that made my life worth living? Up there in that unreal world of theirs, Cupid had hung up his bow, True Love had given up waiting and gone home to its cold lonely bed, poor old St Valentine had been given the sack.

I suddenly felt sorry for Los. I felt sorry for all of them. All those perfect beautiful people. They didn't seem real somehow. No, worse. They were real all right. Real people but trapped in a life story that could never have a happy ending.

20

.

With determination I turned my back on the Tower. In the distance, on a particularly huge and undesirable pile of rubbish, I could see small figures foraging – Downside kids. They'd seen where I'd come from and came running over.

'Chips, chips,' they begged. They were two little boys; they stood, holding out their grubby hands.

I reached in my pocket and brought out a couple of the chips Los had given me.

Their faces were immediately wreathed in smiles.

'Where is this?' I asked.

'Londown.'

'I know, but *whereabouts* in Londown?'

The boys shrugged as if they didn't know what I was asking. 'Big Tip,' said one of the boys, pointing to the mountain of rubbish.

I shook my head. 'No, I mean, what district? Mayfair, Notting Hill, Chelsea?'

They just shook their heads and laughed.

'There must be something left,' I said. 'I know, what about the river? The river must still be here.'

'River?' asked one of the boys, frowning.

'You know, water, boats, bridges. The Thames.'

'Oh, Thames, yes, come,' said the other boy and took me by the hand.

The boys led me round a sort of goat path that skirted the rubbish tip and across a pasture where cows were grazing and came to a halt on the edge of a bank. I looked down. Below us, clogged with cow parsley and rampant London pride, was a flat expanse of land that led across to a further bank. In the centre a huge steel pipeline snaked across and disappeared into the base of the Tower.

'The Thames,' said the boys, pointing at the pipeline. So the Upsiders had filched the Thames. Like everything else that was worth anything, the water had gone Upside.

The boys obviously thought that information had earned them their chips and ran off leaving me there.

I stared down at 'the Thames' and suddenly felt a wave of homesickness for its familiar murky waters. I thought of the walks I'd had with various boys beside it. Although admittedly some of those had been a *real* mistake. I thought of the first kiss I'd had with Los way back, I mean *centuries* back, in 1997 in the dawn, on the bridge, with the river sliding silently beneath us. He'd tried to tell me then that we didn't have any future. But I hadn't listened.

Oh why had I embarked on this insane trip?

There was no way I could get back home unless I could get back Upside. But there was no point in trying the route I'd come by. That led straight into a hotbed of RPs. I'd have to find an alternative way. But how would I ever find it in time? There were only a few hours to go until six o'clock. I started wandering frantically along the dried-up riverbank in the unlikely hope that I'd come across some accessible, unguarded and unthreatening way up.

If only I hadn't been de-wired I could cross-post with Los.

If only I could e-mail him. If only I could e-mail *anyone*. Like Chuck, for instance, he'd be bound to think of something. He'd promised to be my back-up. And then I remembered, guiltily, that I still hadn't tracked down his blasted equation.

There was a ragged shantytown of turf-covered dwellings up ahead. I decided to make for that in the hope of finding some sort of method of communication.

The place seemed deserted apart from one old woman who sat at the pathside washing potatoes in a muddy wooden bucket. A lonely-looking goat tethered to a tree bleated balefully at me. I could hardly picture an Internet Café emerging like an oasis through the woodsmoke. Even a couple of cocoa tins on a piece of string was probably too state of the art round here.

I nodded at the woman and she smiled a gap-toothed smile at me. They didn't even have decent dental care – God this whole place was ghastly.

As I left the village and struck out into open country I was overcome with this huge tidal wave of homesickness. I thought longingly of our fridge stocked with Fruit Corners and Scotch pancakes and of our pantry, with my hidden stash of milk chocolate Digestives and my jumbo box of Coco Pops. I thought of our bathroom, with all the clean fluffy towels and the instant hot water and my favourite shampoo and conditioner. I thought of my bed with Fred Bear waiting for me in it. God I was tired. I even thought nostalgically of Daddy's Apple Mac, sitting on his desk in his study and I felt sorry for the way I'd maligned it last time I'd used it.

And then it occurred to me that I could find my home if I wanted to. I only had to follow the riverbed and it would lead me there. But which way? Was I currently north or south of the river?

How I wished I had one of those books that tells you amazing facts about which side moss grows on trees or how to work out your direction by the angle of your shadow at particular times of day. But I suppose it wouldn't have been much help really because I hadn't got a watch so I had no idea what time of day it was.

I stumbled on blindly through waist-high grass and over tilting paving slabs, finding stray bits of asphalt which showed where roads had once been, and great tangled masses of brightly coloured debris which showed where shops had once been. Once I came across a last lost petrol station, the skeletons of its pumps still standing in age-blackened rows like totems to some long-lost religion.

I didn't really know what I was looking for since all the buildings I would normally have used as landmarks had fallen down. But I followed the riverbed nonetheless. At one point, as I forced my way through dense undergrowth, I came across a rusting pile of swings in what must once have been an inner city park. Some metres further on, I was picking my way over a particularly rough pile of rusted metal when I noticed something golden glinting in the rubble. I knelt down, it was the head of a Buddha, half-buried, looking back at me with its eternal smile still intact.

It was the shrine! Surely there could only be one by the river. The one they'd built in Battersea Park back my time. I rose slowly to my feet. Yes, sure enough there was something familiar about the angle of the Embankment opposite me. There was the bend where the houseboats had been moored. I could still make out the rotting hulk of one of them, lying like some vestige of a Viking longboat in the mud.

I struggled down into the riverbed. Trees had grown up rampantly across it, cutting off the view of the further side. I scrambled my way through, relying on instinct, hoping I could sense the way home like a homing pigeon.

Once up on the further bank I found piles of rubble which

suggested where a terrace of houses must once have stood. I could just make out which was the last house in the terrace. Could this be our house? Number 122? Bits of rotting timber showed where it had been shored up. What was left of the lower walls now sagged drunkenly and the front railings had rusted to a fine coating of red dust.

But the York stone front steps were still virtually intact. With a beating heart I scrabbled in the grass. Pulling back a tuft, I came across a slab with a crack in it which was the shape of a dog's head. How many thousand times had I crossed that step? Up and down the stairs, jumping that one so as not to tread on the dog's head. It was my front step all right.

Searching through the debris, I came across our brass knocker, all green with verdigris and rusted almost beyond recognition. And beside it there was a gleam of something bright blue shining through the grass. I pulled back a tussock and rubbed it clear with my hands. It was a blue Heritage plaque which bore the eerie message:

Justine Duval
1981–
Pioneer Time-traveller
lived here

I sat, gazing at the plaque, having deep and meaningful thoughts. Justine Duval. Duval, now that was not such good news, unless I was using my maiden name professionally, like teachers did at school when they got married – so as not to confuse everyone. Pioneer Time-traveller. *Time-traveller*. Hadn't I done anything else? What had happened to that brilliant movie career I'd planned for myself? Or all those albums I was intending to record . . . My eye returned in a rather spooky way to 1981– . . .

It was the gap after the dash that was worrying. Maybe I'd

never got back. I tried to work out by the angle of the sun what the time might be. The minutes must be ticking away to six o'clock. The shadows were getting ominously long. Maybe I'd got marooned Downside for ever. Perhaps I'd starved to death on some festering rubbish dump.

I cast around for the kind of nutritious nuts or berries or mushrooms that people in those ecological programmes always seem to find burgeoning out of the ground and providing delicious free sustenance wherever they happen to be.

No such luck. There was only one really poisonous-looking toadstool and nothing else to eat except grass.

If only I could get in touch with Chuck. I stared at the ground, wishing, as if by some miracle I'd find Daddy's Apple Mac sticking up out of the rubble, still intact, still functioning, still plugged in. Some hope!

Since there wasn't any electricity any more, all that stuff would be useless anyway. Worse than useless. Obsolete. Antique. Positively prehistoric. What did people do with obsolete technology?

That's when I remembered the Science Museum. I used to go there with Daddy on wet Sunday afternoons, when he was trying to make up for not getting involved in my education. I'd dutifully observe all the exhibits with a suitably awed and fascinated expression, and then we'd go and have a slap-up tea at a tea-shop in South Kensington.

They had the first telephone in the Science Museum, and the first rocket . . . And the very first adding machine that had ever been made. Surely they must have a computer?

I wondered if a Downside museum could possibly yield such up-to-date technology as they had back my time. Except that it wasn't up to-date in this millennium, of course. Knowing my luck, it was probably so old hat they'd have chucked it out. But it was worth a try.

21

Time was ticking by. It seemed to take for ever to track my way to the museum. But at last I saw the building through the trees. Parts of the Gothic roof had disappeared but the stone walls still stood, raggedly like battlements, silhouetted against the sky. The plinth over the entrance was intact and bore the words *Science Museum* deeply engraved in the stone.

The grand mahogany entrance doors were rotting on their hinges. They creaked eerily as I pushed my way in. I found the interior shrouded in darkness and as the doors slammed behind me, they made a hollow sound that echoed as if in a church.

I peered into the gloom. Inside, the main gallery seemed to be quite miraculously just as I remembered it. The glass cases were still standing there and you could see where someone had been at work cleaning them, making inroads into their soft grey covering of dust. On the nearest of these a stub of candle had been left with a few rough handmade matches laid out beside it. I struck a match and lit it. The flame flickered and then grew, surrounding me in a little area of light. Filmy curtains of cobweb hung across the aisles, and in the glass cases I could now make out the shadowy shapes of the exhibits.

Ancient engines and pumps and mills and various other random examples of the age of steam power loomed like great sleeping monsters just visible in the twilight.

My heart sank. Where did one look for a computer? Where did one begin? I held my candle up high and started to make my way through the gallery.

The rooms that led off were all systematically numbered and dated. At the far end I came across a side gallery which was marked *Second Millennium*. This looked more hopeful.

The glass cases in this gallery displayed an odd assortment of exhibits. I realised most of them contained stuff that had been dug up by fossickers. In the first, under the heading Ancient Ancestor Worship there was a display of golf-ball shaped soaps and a hideous rayon tie and handkerchief set – sad relics from the long redundant Father's Day. Further on there was a vintage Teasmade and a collection of caddies, strainers and teapots accompanied by a long and worthy screed of the evils of tea drinking.

I came to a halt at the end of the gallery.

I was face to face with a big mahogany display board, like the one we had at school which listed all the preppy swots who'd got degrees at decent universities. It said, engraved in gold letters:

MCM–MM
NOBEL CLONES
*The following persons have been awarded the ultimate accolade
in recognition of their contribution to human knowledge.*

Below this was a long list of names in alphabetical order. Automatically I cast an eye down the list, just in case my name should be on it. Well, I had a blue plaque, didn't I? No such luck. Nothing between Dawkins and Hawking.

There was a cough at my elbow.

I jumped and swung round to find a balding man in a brown overall standing by my side. He was leaning on a broom. He looked like a janitor.

'Not disturbing you, am I? I was gonna clean up a bit,' he said.

'No . . . not at all. Do you work here? Maybe you could help.'

'Do what I can. We don't get many visitors these days.'

'You see, I'm trying to track down a computer.'

'Just getting round to dusting them this very morning, I was,' he said.

He led me further on to where there was a whole set of display cases devoted to the 'Dawn of the Information Era'. Inside the first there was an old PC with most of its keys missing, beside that was an iMac, its blue plastic casing now cracked and brittle, opaque with age, and further still a laptop so small it was more like a palmtop. Beyond that, there were things so flat and featureless I was totally at a loss to know what they were.

'Do they work?' I asked.

He sucked through his teeth and looked at me suspiciously. 'Now what would you be wanting them to work for?'

'I'm trying to get in touch with someone Upside.'

'Boyfriend, is it?'

I nodded. 'Yes.'

He shook his head firmly. 'Thought it might be something like that. Sorry, miss. It's more than my job's worth. Now if it was anything else I could help you with . . .'

'No . . . No, I don't think there is.' I turned away. But hang on, this was a Science museum, wasn't it? 'Unless, of course, you could help me find an equation.'

'An equation?'

I had a sense that maybe I wasn't talking to entirely the right person. I mean, it wasn't exactly the kind of thing you were likely to come across while dusting glass cases.

'It's probably in a book, somewhere. Do you have a library?'

'A book?' he repeated, even more doubtfully.

'No books?'

'I think we might have had one once. But you know books – last one we had fell apart. What kind of an equation was it?'

With one tremendous effort I remembered what Chuck had asked for. I let it out all in one breath: 'The-complete-unifying-theory-of-the-universe.' (I got it right first time!)

'Oh that!' he said. 'Easy! Everyone knows that! Why didn't you say?'

He started to write laboriously on the dust in the top of the display case.

'$E = mc^2 +$,' he paused. 'No, that wasn't it. Hang on a mo . . . Yeah, $E = mc^2 + V(n2 - pi^2)$, erm . . .'

By the time he'd finished, the equation was so long it went right across the entire surface of the case.

'Are you absolutely sure?'

'Positive. First thing we learn in junior school. Can't even begin on Astrophysics without that.'

I stared at the equation. I'd never memorise that in a thousand years. Every movement I made was in danger of shifting the dust. I hardly dared to breathe.

'I suppose you haven't got a pen on you, have you?'

'Pen?' he looked amazed.

'Or a pencil would do and maybe some paper?'

'Paper? Last bit we had completely disintegrated, sorry.'

'Nothing I could write on?'

He coughed and more dust flew off, almost erasing the last few symbols of the equation.

'Unless . . .' he paused, jingling the keys in his pocket. 'Unless, of course, there was a bit of juice left in one of those.' He nodded in the direction of the computer cabinets.

'Juice?'

'Power. I'm not strictly meant to do this, but it's worth a try.'

He went over to the cabinet with the miniature palmtop in it and unlocked the glass lid. He polished it with his sleeve. 'Amazing the stuff they dig up, isn't it? Must be well over nine hundred years old. Now, if I'm right in thinking, if we open it up . . .' He drew a rusty penknife out of his pocket and eased it into the side. Sure enough, it split open. 'OK, watch this. This is the power chip. Not many people know this trick.'

He slid the chip out of the back and warmed it over the candle flame.

'Now I'll pop it back in and if you're quick about it, you should be able to punch something in?'

I stared as the tiny screen leaped into life. With a shaking hand I fed in Chuck's e-mail number. It was working! My hands were shaking as I started to type.

$E = mc^2 + V(n2 - pi^2) \ldots$

The screen flickered and dimmed but I continued to the end of the equation. There was still some life in it, so I added:

Jx
Science Museum
London 3001
HELP!

Then with my heart in my mouth, I clicked Send. At that moment the powerchip failed. Had my message arrived or hadn't it?

There was a dull slam of a door in the distance.

'Oops!' said the janitor. 'Better get a move-on, or I'll be in trouble.'

Deftly, he slipped the palmtop back in the glass case and locked it. He set about sweeping the floor whistling to himself.

I heard footsteps crossing the gallery. I could dimly make out a figure.

'A'ernoon, prof,' said the janitor without looking up.

'Who's that?'

'Prof Davis. Bit of a boffin. But he's OK.'

The prof had reached the main doors by this time and as he opened them a stray ray of sunlight fell across his face.

It couldn't be. It was. This was impossible.

'Chuck!' I screamed.

The figure turned and peered into the gloom.

'Who's there?'

I was running across the gallery by this time.

'Chuck. It's me. Justine!' I arrived breathlessly at the doorway. 'Chuck! How on earth did you get here?'

He was standing, holding the door open, waiting for me.

'I'm sorry . . .?' he said, looking at me blankly.

'Look! It's me, Justine . . .'

What was the matter with him? He didn't seem to recognise me. He had this really odd, puzzled expression on his face. The way he was staring at me really freaked me out.

'Oh-my-god! You're not Chuck, are you?' I said, slowly coming to my senses.

'Chuck?'

'Chuck Davis?'

'You don't mean Charles Nevil Davis?'

'Yes!'

'Well, yes and no.'

'What do you mean?'

'Come with me,' he said, beckoning to me.

He led me back across the gallery. My candle still stood on the glass case, casting its shifting shadow over to where my friendly janitor was now at work polishing the Board of Nobel Clones with a soft rag.

'You see,' said the professor, pointing up at the board.

I looked up to where he was directing my gaze. The name Charles Nevil Davis had appeared written directly above Richard Dawkins and Stephen Hawking on the board. I could swear it hadn't been there earlier.

I swung round and stared hard at him.

He smiled and nodded.

'You're a clone,' I said slowly. 'You're a clone of Chuck.'

'Great-great-great-great-clone of the famous Charles Nevil Davis. The physicist who discovered . . .'

I wasn't listening. This was impossible. My mind was skating on the thin ice of credulity doing the equivalent of triple toe-loops.

'That was Chuck. The one I knew . . .' I cut in. I stared hard at him. 'But you're totally identical. This is so-oo freaky.'

'Only as identical as identical twins.'

'But I feel as if I know you.'

'So you're a time-traveller . . . fascinating. When do you come from? It must be really early on . . .'

'Nineteen ninety-eight.'

'You're not *the* Justine . . . Justine Duval? The pioneer . . .' It was his turn to be amazed now. 'Justine Duval, I've so much to ask you.'

'Yes, that's me,' I said. 'But listen, you've got to help me. You see, I'm meant to go back to my time tonight.'

'Tonight?'

'By six. There's a time-slot booked.'

'By six! Oh dear. You'd better come to my office.'

22

Chuck's, or should I say Chas's office contained enough obsolete electronic hardware to stock a couple of PC Worlds. Everywhere there were toppling mountains of grimy components. He must've had a small army of fossickers digging them up. I picked my way through a tangled undergrowth of fibre optic cables.

'So you actually knew the famous C.N.D.? Tell me, what was he like?' Chas was asking.

I stared at the worktable, which had the guts of several computers spewing out across it. A manky apple core had got itself entwined with the cables.

'He was just like you,' I said.

'Really?' he said. 'Wicked.'

He swept a pile of circuit boards off a stool to make room for me to sit down.

'But listen,' I said. 'I can't just sit here. Time's passing. This is really important. Do you think you could get me back?'

'Back?'

'To my time.'

'Your time? Tricky. I mean, the real question is,' he said, 'how did you ever come to be here in the first place?'

I started telling him about Los and how he'd invited me and what a disaster it had all been. He listened, giving an impatient nod from time to time. And then I got to how we were parted. I'm afraid I got a bit maudlin at this point.

Chas looked helpless and passed me a handkerchief. (You see, he was *exactly* like Chuck.)

'But that's not what I mean. What I mean is, *how* did you come to be here? You see, they weren't technologically advanced enough in 1998.'

'But they were. They must have been. They scanned me into this massive scanner thing at this Butrav terminal place . . .'

'Scanner?' he said, getting to his feet. Reverently he lifted a dustsheet off a neighbouring workbench. 'Did it look anything like this?'

Underneath, battered, rusty and caked with verdigris, was a scanner just like the one at Butrav.

'Yes, as a matter of fact. Bit newer-looking, but it was pretty much like that one.'

'If they could get you here, I could get you back. But they couldn't have. They didn't have the software. Not in 1998.'

'But they must have. Or else I wouldn't be here, would I? You know, Justine Duval – time-travel pioneer and all that?'

'But it's impossible. Unless . . . unless . . .' Chas had a distant look in his eyes. 'Unless they were using software from our time. Which they could, in theory, if someone had exported it to them.'

'Who would want to do that?'

'They'd have to be pretty clued up in Infotech . . .' he said, eyeing the range of equipment on his bench. 'And they'd have to have a pretty good reason for getting you up here . . .'

'Like who? No, wait a minute . . .' I was staring at him again. 'Like you . . . Like you and Chuck . . .'

He shook his head. 'Wish we could take the credit for it. We've cracked the power problem – converted one of the coal-burning engines in the gallery to wood. It's been our dream. Everything we've ever lived for. It's taken the lot of us. All seven versions, going all the way back to the great C.N.D. And at last, just this week, I ironed out the final glitches. The DTR programme is ready to run.'

'DTR?'

'Digital–temporal realignment . . .'

'That's what they called it at the terminal.'

He fell silent for a moment, deep in thought. 'But it's not possible. No, couldn't be done. Totally impossible. Unless, of course . . . unless . . . I could export the software back to them before you reached the terminal . . .'

'What?'

'Yeah! They will have logged on the time you checked in. It's just a matter of downloading the software before you were scanned.'

'But that would mean I'd have got here before I'd left, if you know what I mean.'

'Only if you're being really literal.'

'Literal!'

'It's quite simple, really – just a matter of parallel universes, that's all.'

(Don't they always say that when they're trying to blind you with science?)

'We're so close and yet so far . . .' he was muttering to himself. 'Everything's absolutely ready. The only problem is getting those last few chips . . .'

I felt in my pocket. 'Would these help?'

His eyes lit up. With shaking hands he took a small screwdriver out of one pocket and an eye-glass out of the other and examined the chips in the light.

'Oh yeah. These could help all right. These could help! But it may take some time.'

He started to unscrew the back of the nearest and largest computer. Bor–ing. I'd had scenes like this before with Chuck. He'd get his head into some problem and I'd sit there like some vegetable going past its sell-by date, doing nothing whatsoever. I could positively grow mould all over before he remembered I was there.

'Look, if it's going to take ages I might just pop outside for a breath of fresh air.'

But Chas wasn't listening. He was leaning over the console, intent on the work. He was muttering to himself under his breath: 'Yeah, sorted. I could use the DTR entry protocol which would enable me to access cyberspace digitally via cd–dot–wormhole–dot–linx . . .'

He was *exactly* the same as Chuck, *married* to his blasted computer.

23

I walked out of the museum and into the late afternoon sunlight.

What a bummer. I'd come all this way, yet here I was, back where I'd started from, stuck with Chuck, or Chas as he was now called. And what was most galling of all was the realisation that I wouldn't be here at all if it wasn't for them.

And unless they could get me out of this mess it looked like I'd be stranded here – Downside – where it was all grotty and muddy and overgrown and out of date. And my hair was a mess and I was wearing an absolutely ghastly outfit in a colour that I'd never be seen dead in normally.

Oh how had I messed up my life? It had been going so well for a while. If only one could take out all life's off-takes, with all the mistakes and trips and falls, like they do when they make movies. So that you could have one life, expertly edited, seamlessly perfect and building up to an absolutely inevitable happy ending with the right guy by your side.

Sigh.

'Justine!' A voice broke through my train of thought.

I wasn't alone. A figure was standing in the shadows. I shielded my eyes against the low sunlight.

The voice rang out again. 'Justine!'

It had that slight break in it that made my heart turn over.

I hadn't seen him standing there. He must've been watching me. And now he stepped forwards and stood outlined against the sunset. The light was glowing like a halo round his tousled tie-died hair. His eyes were an impossibly deep blue in the half-light.

'Justine!' he said again, more gently this time.

I felt every molecule in my body wake up and shake itself and switch to red alert. Life suddenly went into slo-mo as I walked towards him.

(I don't know about you – but this is what I would call a really romantic moment.)

'Los! What are you doing here?'

'I had to come and find you. I couldn't understand it. I had this terrible pain here . . .' He pointed to his chest. 'I kept on thinking about you. I couldn't get you out of my mind. It was like I was possessed . . . What have you done to me?'

'I haven't *done* anything to you.'

'Yes you have. I kept on getting pix of you in my optical field. I'd erase them and then they'd come back again. But it's getting better now. Now you're here. It's really odd. I can't understand it.'

'Come a little closer.'

'That's better still.'

I put my arms round his neck. 'Are the pix still there?'

'No, not now you're here for real.'

Our lips met. It was an epic kiss, although I say it myself.

'I feel better. The pain's gone completely,' he said, looking amazed. 'What did you do?'

I looked him straight in the eyes. 'You just caught me in time. I was leaving. Going back home to my time.'

'But you can't. You can't leave me here.'

'Why not?'

'Because . . . Because . . I'll die. I can't live without you.'

'Nonsense, 'course you can.'

He slumped down on a pile of rubble, miserably fiddling with the laces of his moon boots. I sat down beside him.

'Look,' he said. He took a metal ear-stud out of his pocket. 'I've been carrying this around. It's from when they de-wired you. I found it on the floor. So strange. Just holding it helped, somehow.'

I couldn't help smiling. 'Just holding a little ear-stud helped?'

'I know, weird, isn't it?

'They've de-wired you too,' I said, noticing for the first time the little holes in his ears.

He shook his head. 'No, I did it. It was the only way to get down here to find you without being monitored.'

'How did you know where to look?'

'I got this e-mail, said you were at the Science Museum and to get over there urgently, matter of life and death.'

'Who from?'

'I dunno, whoever it was added a TLA that was new to me.'

'Like what?'

'CND.'

'*Chuck.*'

(So he'd brought us together after all. Who would've thought it? – after he'd been so-oo negative about Los. I owed him one. But hey! Think about it. What was I doing for him?)

'It was that guy of yours back home, wasn't it? The geek in the crap hat.'

I nodded. 'What if it was?'

'Don't go back to him,' he said. 'Stay here.'

'You know we wouldn't be allowed back Upside.'

'We could stay down here together.'

'But you'd hate it. It's all cold and smelly and muddy and gloomy and there aren't any games or anything.'

'Not with you, I wouldn't.'

'But I'd hate it. There aren't any shops or clubs or cafés or nice clothes . . . or . . . *anything* . . .'

'Justine,' he said, looking me straight in the eyes: 'I thought you said you loved me?'

This incredibly poignant moment was interrupted by Chas, who came tearing through the undergrowth. I'd never seen anyone so excited before.

'I've done it! It works! The scanner. I've exported the DTR programme and it works! Right back in 1998. It means you're right. You are the first pioneer. And now I can send you back. It's just a few minutes to six. We can use the same time-slot!'

I got to my feet. 'I've got to go.'

'What if I came with you?' asked Los.

'But you'd hate it. It's all so backward and boring and old-fashioned . . .'

'No I wouldn't. Not with you, I wouldn't. I'd go anywhere with you.'

I hesitated.

He stood there, looking absolutely adorably helpless. 'Justine,' he said. It was almost a whisper.

'What?'

'I . . .'

'Mmm?'

'I think . . .'

'You think . . .?'

'No, I know. I know I do.'

'What?'

'I love you, Justine.'

I tried not to smile but I couldn't help myself: 'But I thought you said there was no such thing as love.'

24

You know how, on those real turning points in your life, you can somehow stand back and watch yourself? Well, that's how it was at that moment.

Los took my hand in his and he locked his fingers through mine and held them tight so that I couldn't pull away if I tried. (Not that I was trying anyway.)

And as the sun dipped towards the horizon we walked together back into the museum. The last that was seen of us in the year 3001 was our shadows thrown long on the pathway, which mingled into one as we passed through the doorway.

As the museum clock struck six we were already on our way back to a time when we could be together. Our time.

Sigh . . .

Oh, and by the way . . .

If you want to know what happened next, you'll have to surf our website:

JUSTINE and LOS@

http://ourworld.compuserve.com/homepages/cyberia